Dusted Star

Masters of the Prairie Winds Club

Book Ten

by Avery Gale

Prologue

LAKYN CURSED THE piece of shit rental she'd driven halfway across the country. The car looked great when she'd picked it up, but she quickly discovered a great-looking exterior didn't mean it was solid on the inside. *There's some irony for you! Hell, you'd think I'd have already figured that out.* She swore the only thing her parents ever agreed on was that she was their best bet for fame and fortune... evidently, it didn't matter if they were only living vicariously.

Her older brother, Cooper was the only reason her parents hadn't managed to spend every nickel she'd ever earned. Seven years her senior, Cooper had been as gifted academically as she'd been physically. He'd called his parents bluff when he had been twelve, threatening to turn them into the authorities if they didn't establish a trust fund for her earnings. Cooper had accused them of blatantly exploiting their only daughter and threatened to go to the local paper as well. Their parents had known he wasn't bluffing and reluctantly established a trust to manage her six-figure income.

She'd heard the story so many times, it was easy to take his remarkable behavior for granted, but anyone who knew her brother now wouldn't be surprised to learn he'd been resourceful enough to make good on his threats. The simple fact was Cooper had always been more of a parent to her than their actual parents.

When they died in a small plane crash a few weeks before her seventeenth birthday, Cooper had, somehow, persuaded his commanding officer to send him home for an unprecedented extended leave. Her brother arrived in time to make all the arrangements for the funerals and then somehow Cooper had managed to persuade Uncle Sam to let him stay long enough to act as her guardian until she could be declared a legal adult by the courts.

The irony was she'd already been living on her own in New York City for almost a year when her parents passed. They'd happily rented her a small apartment and stepped aside, content spending the money she sent them each month. Lakyn had worked seven days a week, so there hadn't been any real need for their parental guidance, but she'd still felt the loss to the bottom of her soul when they died.

After living independently for so long, it had seemed more than a little odd to be forced to wait for the court to tell her she was capable of doing what she'd already *been doing* for almost a full year. As it turned out, the bigger irony was, in the end, the court had been the only one who considered her an adult.

Cooper had a micromanaged her career and safety from the other side of the globe. He'd helped her renegotiate her modeling and acting contracts, and she'd continually been astonished at how easily her manager had bowed to Cooper's decisions. The asshole's percentage was cut almost in half, but her earning potential was so much higher, she knew he'd seen a substantial increase in his bottom line.

She often wondered why she continued paying Reggie when she and her brother had done a better job, and

Cooper was rarely in the country. Even though the entire process was exasperating at times, she'd never questioned her brother's motives. Cooper was the one person who loved her unconditionally... he always had, but Lakyn would be the first to admit, there were times, his unrealistically high expectations were tough to live up to.

Groaning when the car shuddered with what Lakyn feared was a death rattle, she pulled onto the shoulder of the road, just as all the electronics blinked out. Thank God she was on flat ground because as it turned out, her knowledge of cars was seriously lacking. Who the hell knew you lost the power steering and brakes when the vehicles' brain short-circuited. *Don't be a dork, girl. You haven't even seen an ant hill for over an hour. Flat doesn't begin to describe this highway. Well, fuck a duck, now I'm talking to myself.*

According to her phone's mapping app, she was really close to her destination. *Really close.* She'd just lock up the car and walk. Lakyn wasn't afraid of walking. She walked all the time in the city, and since she hadn't met any cars for a while, it didn't seem likely her luggage was in any great danger of being stolen.

When the car rocked to the side from the wind, she shuddered and pulled her jacket from the backseat. She watched as what looked like a small bush rolled across the highway and made a mental note to avoid playing any game with Mother Nature that would make her a pin in some crazy cosmic bowling match. Taking a last look in the mirror, Lakyn smoothed her hair before opening the car door. *How bad could it be?*

Chapter One

I T WAS OFFICIAL, Lakyn had lost her ever-loving mind. Dropping to knees, she cursed the day she'd read her first erotic novel. How could one damned hot story lead to her death by sand-blasting? It defied logic.

She'd chatted with a couple at the diner where she'd eaten the best breakfast she'd ever had—*who knew greasy food was so tasty?* They'd warned her it was supposed to be breezy today. *Breezy? What the ever-loving hell? No one said anything about a hurricane. Holy fucking wind tunnel, Batman, this is nuts. At this rate, there won't be any need to worry about being recognized because I'm not going to have any skin left.* She'd heard about the wild Texas wind, but she'd never imagined anything like the gale threatening to sandblast the top several layers of skin from her body. *Should have stayed in the car. Should have stayed in the car. Shit. Shit. Shit. Why didn't I stay in the fucking car?*

After three days of traveling without stopping for more than a couple hours cat-nap, Lakyn knew she was running on fumes, and that was when she always made her worst decisions. Piss her off and she could make solid choices like a military strategist, but exhaustion? Give it up. She couldn't decide her way out of a wet paper bag.

On the rare occasions Lakyn traveled alone, she'd learned stopping to rest invariably led to more problems than it solved. Hotel staff and guests with cell phones were her worst nightmare. If they weren't snapping her picture, they were alerting their friends to her presence, and within minutes, the place was crawling with photographers and fans. It baffled her how strangers, who weren't expecting to see a celebrity in their midst, instantly knew who she was. Hell, she barely recognized herself without all the crap the studio's makeup artists plastered on her face. When she looked in the mirror, she saw Lakyn Hicks, but the rest of the world saw Lakyn Storm.

Yes, indeed, Reggie Parks was going to stroke out when he discovered she'd slipped out from under his watchful eye. Her manager rarely let her out of his sight long enough for Lakyn to take a deep breath. He claimed her brother had charged him with her safety, but she knew better. He was like a kid guarding his lunch ticket... any concerns he had about her safety were directly linked to his bank balance. Why had Cooper hired the hulking shadows to follow her around each time she left her apartment if Reggie was supposed to be protecting her? *Protecting me, my ass. More like Scrooge guarding his investment.*

Cooper was going to be seventy kinds of pissed off as well because she'd given his guys the slip twice in the past week... but she didn't care. She'd needed a break, and the woman she'd been talking to online had graciously offered her a place to stay if she was ever in Texas. They'd become fast friends when they discovered they had mutual friends and shared interests. Of course, Tobi West only knew her as the younger sister of one of her husband's former teammates, but in Lakyn's view that made their connection all that more significant because it was real. *I hope she doesn't think I misled her... but I guess I did. Damn, is this fucking wind ever going to stop? Think about something else, Lakyn... anything else.*

Lakyn loved her brother to distraction, but she wasn't naïve. Cooper was a player of the first order. Any woman who got involved with Cooper Hicks was doomed to heartache and probably more than a little kink for her trouble. She'd figured out her brother was a Dom after reading her first BDSM novel.

Rolling her eyes at her own distraction, Lakyn couldn't help but wonder how long she was going to be forced to listen to her brother lecture her when he discovered she'd given his security detail the slip and driven across country alone. *Face it brother, mine… if I can slip past them, you weren't getting much for your money, anyway.*

For some reason, Lakyn still couldn't wrap her head around that Cooper was convinced she was still the same girl who got lost in the woods behind their family home when she'd been little more than a toddler. It had been ten-year-old Cooper who'd found her battered and bruised at the bottom of a small ravine. He'd carried her up the steep incline and over a mile before other searchers spotted them and pulled her from his exhausted arms. In Cooper's mind, Lakyn would always be the helpless little child he'd carried to safety.

Shaking her head, she blinked as beads of sweat rolled into her eyes. Hiding beneath her heavy jacket had seemed like a great idea when all she'd been worried about was the vicious sting of blowing dirt. Now, she wondered if it was possible to suffocate under a lined nylon jacket. Suddenly, using the coat as a shelter didn't seem like the stroke of genius it had a few minutes ago. *I should have stayed in the damned car.*

Juan Rivera looked out over the wind-swept prairie and sighed. "Fuck I need a break. Another rescue like the last one and I'm going to turn into the biggest pussy on the planet." His long-time friend, Trac Hughes rolled his eyes and shook his head.

"Don't try to sell that unaffected attitude bullshit to me, man. The conditions we found those kids in got to every man on the team." It was the truth. Every member of the team had crashed hard as soon as they'd returned to Prairie Winds.

"Yeah, well, seeing anyone chained to a damp wall and covered in their own excrement will give you pause." Trac's cool assessment didn't fool Juan, he'd seen the horrified look on his friend's face when they'd stepped through the barn doors. The worst had been the knowledge they'd been so damned close to home. Discovering representatives from a slave-trading organization, headquartered in the Eastern Block, had somehow managed to establish a holding facility less than five hundred miles from their front door had been damned humbling.

Juan frowned when the visibility dimmed to less than a quarter mile. "Fucking dust, I hate not being able to see what's coming at me." Squinting, he slowed to get a better look at a dark sedan, sitting too close to the edge of the road. "What the hell? Who leaves their fancy ass car on the side of the road in this wind? There won't be a speck of paint left on the passenger's side by morning."

"I didn't see anybody in the car. They probably caught a ride and called for their auto club. Hell, nobody with any sense would try to walk in this wind. You know this is blowing up a fucking storm. Keep going, I want to get back to Prairie Winds before we get hammered."

Biting back his laughter, Juan had lost track of how

many times he'd reminded his friend not everyone had the same level of understanding of everyday situations. Trac had zero-tolerance for what he considered a lack of common sense.

Juan continued driving, but something about the abandoned car keep niggling in the back of his mind. A couple of miles down the road, the hair on the back of his neck began standing on end as he fought to see through the blowing dust crossing the highway in reddish-brown clouds. He barely caught a glimpse of what looked like someone dropping to the ground before his view was once again obscured by the dark cloud of moving dirt. Slowing, he edged closer to the side of the blacktop, careful not to run over whatever was huddled a few yards ahead.

"What the hell is that?" Trac was leaning forward as Juan jumped from the truck as soon as it rocked to a stop. As Juan approached, he could hear a muffled voice, but whoever was hiding beneath what looked like a winter coat didn't respond when he asked if they needed help. *Who the hell wears a winter coat in Texas?*

The question was quickly erased from his mind when he knelt close, blocking as much of the wind as possible and lifted the corner of the dust-covered coat. Looking down, he found himself gazing into the most beautiful eyes he'd ever seen. The unique striations of deep blue reminded him of the violet lilacs his mother loved so dearly, but those distinctive outer rings faded to the palest blue he'd ever seen. The effect was haunting, and his breath caught when the woman blinked in surprise that quickly morphed to fear when he didn't speak for several seconds. Before Juan managed to speak, Trac's booming voice sounded over the howling wind.

"What the fuck, Rivera? If it's a critter, you're not picking it up. No more fucking strays, our place is already a damned zoo." As a former Special Agents with the FBI, he and Trac had worked together for longer than Juan wanted to think about, so there was no reason to deny his soft heart when it came to animals in need. Giving a startled yelp, the angel with the beautiful eyes pulled the coat back over her, quickly ducking out of sight.

"Damn it, Hughes, you scared her." *Great, now I find my traitorous voice.*

"Her?"

"Yeah, her as in person. Two legs, not four." Pulling the coat back up, Juan smiled and held out his hand.

"Come, *Chiquita*. Let's get you out of this wind before we all get run over." Standing on the edge of the highway wasn't safe. He was anxious to get back in the truck. The thunderheads were moving in fast, and once the lightning started, the danger of being out in the open would increase exponentially.

Juan was relieved when she finally slipped her small hand into his much larger one. Her fingers were so delicate in his palm, he was worried about crushing them just by pulling her to her feet. A white-hot bolt of electricity streaked up his arm at the initial contact, making him suck in a quick breath, and he knew his eyes had widened in surprise.

Helping her to her feet, Juan had the strangest feeling he'd seen her somewhere, but her face was so smudged with dirt, it was difficult to tell. She was petite, the top of her head barely reaching his shoulder, and she was wearing a ridiculous pair of heels. When she stumbled against him, murmuring an apology, he heard Trac swear, "Holy shit."

Before Juan could ask Trac what was wrong, the woman surprised him by asking, "Do you know Tobi West?"

When he and Trac both stopped and stared at her, the woman ducked her head and grimaced. "Sorry, I was hoping perhaps you knew how close I was to her house. She told me if I was ever in Texas, I was welcome, and well, I was hoping to surprise her. She said her place was... well, special. You know and... safe." *Safe?* Why did the angel with the beautiful eyes need a safe place?

Without answering her question, Juan took her hand in his and led her to the truck. Opening the driver's door, he lifted her effortlessly into the center of the seat before getting in beside her.

"Yes, *Cariña*, we know Tobi. We were headed to Prairie Winds ourselves." He wanted to smile at the pink blush that spread beneath the dirt smudges on her cheeks. Obviously, she wasn't completely clueless about the club.

"What's your name, darlin'?" There was an edge in Trac's voice Juan didn't understand, something between amusement and annoyance. Since Trac's southern accent was more pronounced when he was aroused, Juan was going with amused and was relieved to see he wasn't the only one attracted to her.

"Lakyn. Lakyn Hicks." She'd added her last name so quickly, Juan couldn't help glancing over her head at Trac, raising a brow in question. The shit-eating grin on his friend's face should have been a clue, but he honestly had no idea what Trac was smiling about.

"Want to amend that, Princess?" This time Trac's voice definitely sounded amused despite his stern reprimand.

"Damn." Her whispered curse came just as Juan turned onto the long drive leading to Prairie Winds. Pulling to a stop in the recently built parking garage, Juan switched off the ignition and turned in his seat to look at the pair sitting next to him. The smudged angel looked frustrated or guilty, he couldn't decide which, while Trac looked like the cat who swallowed the fucking canary.

Juan had been mildly annoyed a heartbeat earlier because he hated feeling like an outsider looking in, but the defeated look spreading over her face brought his protective nature surging to the surface.

"Spit it out, *Cariña*." Juan's words might have been laced with a sweet Spanish endearment, but there would be no mistaking it for anything other than the command it had been. Rather than answering him, she looked at Trac.

"Do you think she'll be angry?" Now it was Trac's turn to look confused.

"You mean Tobi doesn't know who you are?" She shook her head, and Trac leaned his head back and laughed out loud. "Oh, this just keeps getting better and better."

Juan was losing patience with the side conversation, and his snarl of frustration drew his friend's attention. Nodding in his direction, Trac grinned.

"Juan Rivera, meet Lakyn Storm."

Lakyn Storm? Fucking seriously?

Chapter Two

KYLE WEST LEANED back against his desk, arms crossed over his muscular chest, and shook his head. When he'd gotten the report from Micah Drake a few weeks ago about an ongoing online conversation between his sweet wife and a woman in New York City, he'd been shocked to learn her identity. Not only was the young woman one of the most recognizable faces in the world, she was also the younger sister of one of the men he and his brother had been trying to recruit for the past year.

"Seems like an odd coincidence, doesn't it?" As the head of their cyber-security team, it was Micah's job to know who was talking to whom, and he was damned good at his job. Of course, the man was probably due a healthy bonus for his commitment to keeping the trouble magnet Kyle and Kent called their wife and sub from becoming a target for every bleeding heart on the internet.

"As a rule, I don't believe in coincidences, but something about this woman seems oddly genuine. I'm not sure how to explain it, but I've read and re-read all of their communication, and I've gotten the impression she sees herself as Lakyn Hicks, not Lakyn Storm. I guess we'll see soon enough," Kyle wondered aloud, shaking his head and pushing away from the desk as he watched the trio making their way through the parking garage. It would take them a couple of minutes to navigate the long hall leading to the club's front entrance, but he planned to be on hand to greet them. "It's going to be interesting to find out how she ended up with those two."

"No shit, but from the sappy look on Juan's face, I'm betting he doesn't let her wander far." Kyle agreed with Micah's observation, but he was even more intrigued by Trac's obvious amusement. "Coop's going to owe you big time." Micah's statement of the obvious made Kyle chuckle to himself, and he didn't bother trying to hold back his satisfied smile.

This was leverage most team leaders dreamed of, and he certainly wasn't above using it to his advantage. There were obvious challenges inherent in exploiting a friendship his wife clearly enjoyed, even if they two women had never met face to face, but she was in deep enough, he wasn't going to lose any sleep over it.

Moving to the door, Kyle didn't bother asking if Kent was on his way. Their twin connection was as strong as it had ever been, and Kyle knew his younger brother was already headed to the office. They might only be minutes apart in age, but Kyle had always taken his role as the *elder brother* seriously—too seriously if you asked Kent. He'd take the lead during this little meet and greet, then he and Kent would have a come to Jesus meeting with Tobi.

"Get word to Cooper, let him know we've got her. I'm going to greet our guest."

"When are you going to tell Tobi she's here?" Kyle could hear the underlying amusement in Micah's question. He didn't bother to answer directly because Micah already knew the answer depended on how this encounter went.

"My lovely wife has taken our children over to my parents. Since she and my mom are thick as thieves, I doubt she dropped them at the front door without a gossip session." *Probably putting on the finishing touches to a strategic plan for world domination.* "There is no way my fathers will let her leave with this storm bearing down on us. Hell, I didn't want her to drive over there, but all things considered, I thought it was best for her to be off-site." Even though she was less than a half mile away, it was far enough for right now.

Kyle stepped into the large reception area of the club just as their newest receptionist gasped, "Oh my God, you're—"

He interrupted her before she could alert everyone in the damned place that something was up. Not that it would make much difference with Mikki. Hell, her ever-changing hair color alone drew a ridiculous amount of attention, and the dust-covered star standing in front of him was still easily recognizable despite the layer of grime covering her world-famous face.

JUAN WATCHED AS the petite woman behind the reception desk sprang out of her chair, eyes wide in recognition, her voice sounding more like a cartoon character than the professional air she usually affected. Aside from her ever-changing hair color, Mikki Baxter had proven herself to be remarkably competent from what Juan had observed. She was the first new hire to last beyond her probation period, so the club's members were hopeful Mikki had found a way to deal with Kyle's tendency to intimidate the hell out of submissive employees.

"I'm sure our guest knows who she is, Mikki." Kyle's stern tone made the petite beauty's spine go ram-rod straight. *Okay, so perhaps she isn't immune to the boss after all.*

Juan shook his head and rolled his eyes as he wondered if she'd still be behind the desk tomorrow. It was no wonder the club had gone through a dozen or more receptionists since Rissa officially retired. "Could you please go to the bar and bring our guest a bottle of water?" As soon as she'd gone, Kyle returned his attention to Lakyn.

"Luke has already completed your background check, Miss Hicks." When Lakyn started to speak, Kyle held up his hand, and her mouth slowly closed. Juan would bet she didn't even realize she'd just responded to her first command from a Dominant at the Prairie Winds Club. He frowned, her first command at the club should have come from him, dammit. After all, he was the one who found her along the road. *What the fuck ever happened to finders keepers? Jesus, what's the matter with me?*

"Lakyn, my brother and I are very protective of our beautiful wife. Her open heart and innate trust is a large part of what makes her such a treasure, but it also makes her an easy target, so our security staff helps us keep very close tabs on her."

"It takes a village—a very skilled village to keep Tobi out of trouble." Kent West stepped from behind his brother, flashing his trademark smile, but Lakyn didn't seem to notice the expression Juan suspected had gotten the man endless dates before he and Kyle met Tobi.

"Holy dust bunnies, she wasn't kidding. Tobi said her husbands were mirror image twins, but she insisted she didn't understand why people seem to struggle to tell them… well, you, apart." Lakyn seemed to have completely forgotten Kyle had been speaking to her as she stepped closer to them. Juan hid his grin behind his hand as small poofs of dust followed her movements. Damn if she didn't remind him of Pig-Pen from the old Peanuts gang movies.

Mikki sneezed when she stepped back in the room as dust wafted over the chest-high counter she stepped behind. Lakyn appeared unfazed by the other woman's profuse apology as she held out a small bottle of water.

Watching Lakyn study Kent and Kyle's faces with an unnerving, clinical appraisal edged with appreciation stirred something deep in Juan's core he couldn't quite identify. It wasn't exactly jealousy, but it wasn't joy either. Her scrutiny continued for so long, Kyle appeared to be reaching his saturation point. Juan couldn't remember ever seeing the former team leader so uncomfortable—the whole scene was surreal. She finally stepped back, crossing her dirt-smudged arms over her chest. Juan heard Trac's snort of laughter beside him when another small dust cloud floated around her, sending Mikki ducking behind the counter.

"Your bone structure is nearly identical, and I'd wager your movements, particularly your walks are indeed mirror images… but there are so many subtle differences, I doubt anyone who knows you at all has any trouble telling you apart." The look on Kyle West's face was something between astonished admiration and horrified embarrassment at the impassive assessment from a woman he'd only known less than two minutes.

"Damn, I haven't seen my brother speechless since— well, hell, living with Tobi tends to make that a common occurrence, so I'll qualify it. I haven't seen another woman strike him dumb in a long damned time." Kent's amused tone cut through the escalating tension in the room and sent a sweet flush over Lakyn's dirty cheeks.

"What? Who is this woman who's rendered my Master speechless? I want to meet this wonderful sister of my soul. Keeping two such amazing men in line is exhausting, I could use the help." Tobi's sweet voice floated from behind her men and Kyle's expression immediately softened even though Juan would bet they hadn't planned to introduce the women until they'd had a chance to thoroughly vet Lakyn.

Turning, Kent held out his hand. "Come, kitten, I believe your invited guest has arrived."

"Sweetness, you really should have been more careful with her transportation arrangements. I believe I heard something upstairs about an abandoned car up the road a bit. And from the looks of your chat buddy, she's spent some time out in the wind."

"What? Who on God's green Earth walks in this mess?" Dell West picked his petite daughter-in-law up without blinking and set her behind him, then sidestepped his sons before coming face to face with Lakyn. "Holy fucking hell. Lilly is going to crap a cat." The older man was dressed in his usual jeans and button-down shirt, the gray streaks in his hair making him look like the grandfather he was. Stepping forward, he held out his hand, and Lakyn didn't hesitate to lay her small hand in his. "It's nice to meet you, Miss"

"Hicks, Lakyn Hicks. I'm happy to meet you too, Mr. West." When he looked surprised at her use of his name, she shrugged. "It's easy to see where your handsome sons get their distinguished looks... it was a safe guess."

Tobi squeezed between the men blocking her view with a delighted squeal. "Lakyn? Oh, my stars and garters, I can't believe you're really here." The minute her eyes locked on her long-distance friend, she froze in her tracks.

"Oh shit."

T<small>RAC STOOD QUIETLY</small> to the side, watching everything play out until he saw Lakyn's reaction to Tobi's surprise. Unshed tears filled her eyes and a stark, disillusioned look of rejection moved over her dust-covered face in a sweeping surge. Grasping her shoulders, he slid his hands up until they bracketed her face, focusing her attention on him.

"Darlin', Tobi isn't unhappy to see you, she just knows she's been busted by her Masters." The first tear breached the lower rim of her blue eyes and left a clean stripe of skin as it rolled to her chin.

She gave him an almost imperceptible shake of her head, "It's okay," she whispered, "I'm used to this… really. Could you give me a ride back to my car, please? I'll call a tow-truck and get a motel room for the night, and then figure things out after I've had a good night's sleep."

Trac saw Tobi try to step forward, her eyes wide with guilt, but Kyle's grip around her upper arm halted her progress. It was the first time Trac could remember being genuinely annoyed with his bosses spirited wife. He knew she hadn't meant to hurt Lakyn's feelings, but the pain in the exhausted woman's eyes was gutting him. *Fucking hell, tears are my kryptonite.*

"No, darlin', I'm not going to do that. Let's get you cleaned up and fed, then we'll discuss your options." Before he could move her out of the room, the door opened a fraction, then slammed back shut from the force of the wind. Over the howling squall, Trac heard a string of Spanish curses that would have surely made Columbus' sailors proud.

Juan was already chuckling when he swung the heavy

wooden door open and pulled a petite, dark-eyed ninja into the room.

"Mia, sweetness, why are you coming in this door alone?"

"Fruit fucking salad, I just wanted thirty seconds without those two hovering over me like I was their damned job. Somebody better fix this, or I'm going to start taking boring landscape pictures and hanging them all over the club." Five seconds after she'd finished speaking, the door slammed open again and Tucker Deitz's imposing frame filled the doorway.

"You are in big trouble, Kodak." The man was intimidating on his best days and downright scary dressed in combat and climbing gear as he was now. "I told you I'd walk you up. You've been crawling around a fucking swamp for three days, and suddenly, you can't wait fifteen seconds to get into a shower?" Mia didn't respond, causing Tucker to follow her gaze and flinched when she let out an excited shout.

"Lakyn? Holy margarita magic, what a wonderful surprise." Trac felt Lakyn's quick intake of breath just before the tension seemed to drain from her muscles that had been rigid seconds earlier.

"Mia? Oh my God. You look like a warrior fairy." The two women abandoned the men at their sides and met in the center of the rapidly filling reception area. Their heartfelt embrace emphasized the fact they had obviously met before, their familiarity and friendship were easy to see. Trac wasn't sure why he felt relieved—dammit, he'd promised himself he wasn't going to fall for a woman he knew would leave, and there wasn't a doubt in his mind Lakyn Storm would leave. Hell, her entire life revolved around travel and public appearances.

To the side, Trac noticed Tobi leaning against Kyle who had one arm wrapped loosely around her as he brushed tears from her flushed cheeks with his free hand. Trac knew she felt awful about upsetting Lakyn, and under any other circumstances, perhaps their famous guest might not have reacted so strongly.

It was easy to see Lakyn was running on fumes, the deep purple bruising under her eyes gave away her exhaustion. She'd already been worried Tobi would be angry she hadn't been completely forthright about who she was, so the other woman's response had hit Lakyn hard. There was a part of him that suspected the woman Tobi had been talking to was much more real than Lakyn Storm.

He'd bet his inheritance Tobi had seen deeper into the heart of the real woman than most people were ever allowed to see. Trac wanted to see the transcript of the two women's communication, he suspected it would tell him more about the stunning woman standing a few feet away than anything he could read about her online.

"Someone want to catch me up?" Brock Deitz's deep voice sounded from the door, breaking through Mia and Lakyn's excited chatter. Mia made short work of the introductions and explained the two women had worked together on a couple of projects. They'd become friends but had lost contact over the past several months.

Lakyn reluctantly admitted she'd been forced to change all her online contact information and warning bells were sounding so loud in Trac's mind, he barely registered the rest of the conversation. There were only a few reasons he could think of for a celebrity to suddenly change their contact information, and none of them were good. Hell, the business inconvenience alone had to have been a huge pain in the ass.

Everything he was hearing made him wonder where her manager was while all of this was happening. It seemed to Trac, protecting his client should be a fairly large part of the job description. If Lakyn belonged to him, nothing would come before protecting her. Trac wanted to know why the manager wasn't stepping up to the plate.

Chapter Three

LAKYN LEANED AGAINST the back wall of the elevator and sighed. She was bone-weary and skating on an emotional edge, putting her so close to imploding, a stiff breeze would push her over. Pun intended. She was grateful for the silence of the small space... the howling wind and crashing thunder outside wasn't helping soothe her ragged nerves.

"Okay, my friend. Out with it. What's going on?" Lakyn wasn't surprised by Mia's direct question. Her friend's down-to-earth attitude was one of the things that had drawn Lakyn to her... that and her mad photography skills. The woman had an eye for everything, and Lakyn had never worked with anyone more talented or easier to deal with.

Taking a deep breath, trying to hold back the flood of emotions threatening to pull her under, Lakyn wasn't sure where to start. Damn, the past few weeks had been a nightmare, and she wasn't sure she had the strength to rehash it right now. She needed to shower, eat, and rest before her brain was going to work.

"Listen, I can see you are close to crashing, so let's table this until after we've gotten cleaned up and eaten. I smell like a swamp rat, and you look like a dirtsicle... how did you manage that, anyway?" Before Lakyn could answer, Mia waved her hand and shook her head.

"Never mind, we'll cover that while we eat. I'm so hungry, I'm starting to get dizzy. I haven't had anything good to eat since we left. I swear those Cajuns think all their food has to be floating in spicy soup. I'm dying to eat something I can pick up with my fingers... like a damned cheeseburger and salty fries." When Mia finally paused to take a breath, Lakyn reached out and squeezed her friend's hand.

"Thank you for rescuing me down there. I'd just asked the men who found me to take me back to my disabled car, but I had no idea where I was going to go. I'd been hoping Tobi wouldn't be angry when she learned the woman she'd been talking to online wasn't just Lakyn Hicks, but she took one look at me and muttered a curse, so I doubt it's going to end well."

Of all the responses she might have expected, Mia's howling laughter wouldn't have even made the list. It was obvious her friend was tired, and God knew she did indeed smell like the swamp the man downstairs said they'd been crawling around in. No one had bothered to explain what the mysterious assignment had been, but it had clearly been messy with a side of stench which made Mia's nearly hysterical response even more bizarre.

"Oh, God in heaven, I've missed this place. It's like school, you know? You go every damned day, and nothing happens—not ever. But miss one day and all hell breaks loose, and you're left playing catch-up on the gossip for the rest of the quarter."

Lakyn stood and stared at Mia as she wiped the tears of laughter trailing down her green smudged cheeks. The door of the elevator opened, but Mia halted Lakyn's progress, holding the door open with her other hand.

"I'm sorry. I'm punchy and that hit me funny for reasons you'll soon understand, but you need to trust me, Tobi West is one of the nicest people I've ever met. Her reaction was more likely because she knew she was busted. God only knows why she didn't know Micah and his merry band of computer hackers weren't tracking all her online chatting. Geez, the woman is amazing, but she's also a trouble magnet like no one you've ever met."

Mia's expression had softened to the point it was easy to see she both admired and liked Tobi West. Lakyn took a deep breath and let some of the hesitance she'd felt about staying at the Prairie Winds Club fade away.

"All I'm asking is that you reserve judgment because I promise you, she is beating herself up right now for making you feel unwelcome. If there is one thing I've learned living in Texas, it's how seriously these people take hospitality. I'm convinced it's a part of their DNA."

Lakyn found herself giggling despite the insanity that had decided to take over her life. If her brother would just come back home, things would be better. Cooper had a way of normalizing everything, and she missed him so much, her heart hurt. She'd tried calling all of his usual contact numbers, but no one had seemed remotely interested in tracking him down, just because his sister claimed she needed to talk to him.

The last time he'd re-enlisted, she'd put up a fierce battle, trying to discourage it but ultimately lost. Lakyn knew he was, once again, giving it careful consideration. She was determined to see him out of harm's way even if she had to hire him as her own personal security. There was no question he'd be the best, his training and personal stake alone assured her of that much. But he'd also micromanage her as if she was still the toddler he'd found at the bottom of the ravine rather than the capable adult she'd grown into.

"Come on, you look beat, and I can see your mind is wandering. I recognize that look all too well." Mia led her to the guest suite of the massive apartment she shared at the top of the club. From what little Lakyn had seen, the entire place was magnificent, and she was shocked at the elegance surrounding her.

"Damn, this place is amazing, especially since we're at the top of a sex club."

"Prairie Winds is so much more than just a sex club. You're going to love it here, and whatever it is that sent you running from the city can't get you here." Mia waved her into a bathroom worthy of most of the five-star hotels Lakyn had stayed in. "I'll bring you something to wear and leave it on the counter, so don't lock the door. When you're ready, we'll meet in the kitchen and find us something to eat."

Without another word, Mia disappeared out the door. When she turned to the mirror, Lakyn gave a startled yelp. Her face was so dirty, she barely recognized herself, and her hair looked like she'd stuck her finger in a light socket. The dark circles beneath her eyes made her look like she hadn't slept in a week which wasn't too far from the truth. *Fucking hell, I look like Uncle Fester's evil sister.*

Stripping quickly, she didn't waste any time hitting the shower. It was enormous and beautiful, but Lakyn barely registered her surroundings, preferring to lean against the cool marble wall and let the hot water sluice over her. The massaging jets pounded the top layer of knots from her muscles, causing her to groan so loud, the sound bounced off the walls surrounding her.

It took a substantial amount of shampoo and concentrated effort to get her hair clean. Rolling her eyes, Lakyn wondered what her stylist would say if she could see her using a product that hadn't been *specially formulated* for her hair. Personally, Lakyn still suspected that whole thing was a ruse, and the hundred dollars an ounce shampoo the salon used was being delivered through the backdoor by a camouflaged Dollar General truck.

No matter how much money she earned, Lakyn had never been able to understand the pretenses and nonsense that accompanied having her picture taken and pretending to be someone else. *Yeah, real glad I spent all those late nights studying for my degree.* Cooper had insisted she get a college degree despite the obvious security and attendance issues. It had taken too damned long even with all the *life experience credit* she'd gotten, but she'd finally finished her MBA a year ago.

She wasn't going to admit it to her pushy brother, but the business knowledge she'd gained had already repaid her tuition several times over. She'd renegotiated several contracts and made investments that were already earning her substantial returns. Lakyn had recently renegotiated her manager's contract again and suspected that was a large part of the reason he seemed to be essentially ignoring the problems she'd been having. Once he found out her brother wasn't going to be available to show up unannounced, Reggie had been much too content to sit back and let her do his work.

Lakyn might be a celebrity, but she'd always prided herself on maintaining a strong work ethic. She had little tolerance for laziness, and she damned well didn't intend to fund it. Taking a deep breath, she pushed herself away from the wall. Without opening her eyes, reached for the small bottle of scented body gel she'd chosen from the basket of goodies on the counter and let out a startled scream that reverberated all around her when a warm hand grasped her wrist.

"Be still, *Cariña*. It's just me. I'm here to help. You were in here so long, we became concerned." Juan's smooth, deep voice washed over her like a soft breeze, and her skin tingled as her nipples tightened into stiff peaks. She knew he hadn't missed her reaction when his eyes blazed with heat as they took in her physical response, but he didn't comment. Pouring the exotic smelling gel onto a soft cloth, he started at the top of her shoulders, scrubbing gently.

His touch wasn't overtly sexual, but it was far from clinical. Moving from her shoulders down her back, she groaned as his fingers applied pressure to the tight muscles, kneading the knots until they melted, and she swayed on her feet.

"Put your hands on the wall, baby. I don't want you to fall." It was a good thing she'd braced herself because when he smoothed the soapy cloth over the globes of her ass, her body responded in a whole new way.

"I can smell your arousal, *Cariña*. I can hardly wait to taste your sweet cream, but the first time we make love to you, we want you well rested, so you enjoy each touch," he gave her ass cheeks each a firm squeeze, "and each kiss," he leaned close, pressing his warm lips against the sensitized skin covering her rear, "as much as possible."

Continuing on, he washed the backs of her legs before turning her and reversing his earlier path. When he reached the top of her thighs, he gave the inside a quick tap, and she instinctively moved her legs apart at his unspoken signal.

"More, *Cariña*, don't be shy. I plan to explore every inch of your beautiful body." She moved her legs further apart, bracing herself as he replaced the cloth with his fingers.

"You're so slick, *Cariña,* it's a siren's call to a sexual Dominant, you know. It fills the heart with joy to know the submissive in our care desires our touch, our mastery." Her hips flexed forward of their own volition, and she moaned when he moved his hands up to her lower abdomen. "Not yet, baby—but soon."

Lakyn wanted to demand relief, but she knew he was right, she was much too tired to fully enjoy anything, and a good orgasm might well send her into a coma.

By the time he'd finished, her breasts were tingling and her nipples so sensitive, she was once again unsteady on her feet. She felt him lean past her, and a moment later Lakyn was blasted with cold water. She gasped and nearly fell in her mad scramble to move away from the frigid water. Re-energized when he finally turned the water off, she gave him a rueful, shivering smile when she noticed he was wearing a pair of low slung boxers.

"I feel underdressed for this party." He shook his head and gave her a tender look.

"No, you are dressed perfectly. Believe me, I have nothing but appreciation for your present attire." The heat in his eyes warmed her when it flared in his dark eyes and a muscle in his jaw ticked. It gave her an appreciation for the control he was exhibiting. It was empowering to know he wanted her, but it made her feel safe knowing he was willing to hold back.

"I didn't want to make you any more uncomfortable than was strictly necessary, but *Cariña,* the look of hunger in your eyes is testing my resolve to keep this encounter from drifting to something far more physically taxing, and I know you are not ready. So, it's time to get out of here before I embarrass myself. Come."

After leading her out of the shower, he wrapped her in a towel from the warmer, and Lakyn didn't protest when he began drying her. She'd read enough erotic romance novels and laughed at enough of Tobi's stories to know it would be a wasted effort. One of the biggest draws of the lifestyle, at least for her, was knowing she could step aside and let someone else take control even if it was just for a short while. She didn't want to hand over control in all areas of her life, but it would be nice to have a break every now and again.

Lakyn had been living alone for so long, there were times she worried her window of opportunity to learn how to live with someone else was slipping through her fingers. She wasn't getting any younger, and even she knew her modeling career wasn't going to last forever. Acting would allow her to work a little longer, but it would get harder and harder for her to find great roles in the future. The last thing she wanted was to end up alone.

Everyone believed Lakyn had started acting because she loved performing, but that wasn't true. She'd done it for one reason and one reason only... the money. She didn't crave the attention, she craved financial security. She still found it remarkable what studio executives were willing to pay her to play dress up and pretend to be someone else. Honestly, the entire process reminded her of the games most children outgrew shortly after they started school.

She made an obscene amount of money doing nothing more than having her picture taken and memorizing lines. Lakyn believed in living very conservatively, so her financial future was very close to being locked down. No matter how busy she managed to keep herself, there always seemed to be something missing, and it wasn't until she read her first erotic romance that she'd been able to identify what it was. The first book had awakened something inside her, unlike any book she'd ever read... it had been as if the author had crawled inside her head and taken copious notes before penning the story.

Squeezing her eyes shut to hold back the flood of emotion, Lakyn pulled in several deep breaths to calm her racing heart. The connection she'd felt reading Keme Meadows' books shocked her. Lakyn wasn't a virgin, but the two lovers she'd had several years ago hadn't been any more experienced than she was, and her only two sexual encounters had been woefully unimpressive. By the time she turned twenty, Lakyn had decided a vibrator was a better bet and given up looking for a man who could give her an orgasm.

Meeting Tobi online while trying to contact her favorite author had been a fluke. Tobi had been working on links between Keme's website and several kink clubs around the country when she happened to see Lakyn's posted question pop up on the screen. *There's no such thing as coincidence.* Tobi's words kept playing through her mind, and Lakyn told herself their unlikely meeting had to mean something more.

I sure hope Mia's right about Tobi, and Keme's right about the sex...

Chapter Four

J UAN LISTENED AS Lakyn talked quietly to herself. He tried to fit together the bits and pieces she murmured loud enough for him to hear, but he was coming up with more questions than answers.

He'd been downstairs, standing beside Tucker in Kent and Kyle's office, listening to Kyle explain what little they knew about Lakyn Hicks when the other man's phone vibrated with an incoming text. Mia said Lakyn had been in the shower for so long, she was concerned she might have fallen, but she was uneasy about invading her friend's privacy.

Tucker turned the phone for him to read the message, and Juan quietly slipped out of the meeting and made his way upstairs to check on her himself. Seeing her leaning against the marble wall with her eyes closed as the water cascaded over her bare back and perfectly curved ass, his first thought was she'd fallen asleep, standing up. Stripping down to his boxers, he'd stepped silently into the large enclosure.

He knew he'd startled her and assumed her muted re-action was more likely a testament to her exhaustion than a sign of trust. Feeling her melt beneath his touch as he'd smoothed the soapy cloth over her perfect skin tested his control in ways he hadn't been challenged in years. He managed to keep his cock from claiming too much of his blood flow until he'd seen the desire in her eyes. Christ in heaven, those eyes were going to be the death of him. The banked heat lurking behind the various shades of blue sent a bolt of searing heat from his very core.

There was no question Lakyn Hicks was a beautiful woman. Hell, her face was one of the most recognized in the world, but he suspected few people saw the vulnerability hidden behind the physical perfection. Juan had spent years studying women. He loved the purity of their reactions, especially in those rare moments when they weren't trying to be strong for someone else. He was committed to understanding the correlation between a certain touch and the corresponding response. He loved watching every nuance of their body language as he tried to unravel the mysterious interplay between a submissive's mind and body. Being able to identify subtle changes and interpret even the most elusive signal was the very foundation of BDSM play, in his opinion.

The woman catching fire beneath his touch was inexperienced, and that was a strangely satisfying realization. Since joining the Prairie Winds team, he and Trac had worked personal security for several celebrities, and one of the things that had surprised him the most was how isolated most of their clients felt. The same layers of security insulating them from danger also cut them off from the everyday interactions and experiences the rest of us take for granted. Looking at Lakyn, he wondered now how much she craved normalcy.

Trac loved being in control, it fed his sexual attraction, but Juan was different. For him, the real allure of the D/s kink was as a tool… a means to an end. He didn't care about being in control unless it met the woman's needs.

Juan was the first to admit he was a romantic, a throwback to a time when a woman's gender was something to celebrate rather than defend. Was he old-fashioned? Absolutely. He was also unapologetic about his views— what would be the point? There was no shame in loving women and recognizing them for the wondrous creatures they were.

He wasn't sure what Mia had told Lakyn about Tobi, but he could assure her, it was accurate. In the short time he'd known Mia Mendez, he'd found her to be as open and honest as she first appeared. For a young woman who had been raised in such a privileged environment, she was remarkably down to earth, so he knew anything she'd told Lakyn would be true. Juan also knew Mia and Tobi had become friends, so the Colombian beauty had likely used that angle as well.

Wrapping her in a large towel, Juan realized for the first time how petite she was. *Aren't models usually statu-esque?* Blotting the moisture from the long waves of her chestnut hair, she moaned softly, leaning back into his touch, and he felt another surge of blood abandon his brain and rush to his cock. Thank God he'd replaced his wet boxers with jeans as soon as he'd helped her out of the shower.

"Come." Grasping her hand, Juan led her into the sitting area in the bedroom and settled her on one of the low hassocks. Grabbing the remote, he switched on the fireplace and pulled a wide-toothed comb from his back pocket. "Rest your eyes for a couple of minutes, sweetheart."

"I can comb my own hair, you know. I'm tired, not helpless." He didn't bother to respond for several seconds, letting the silence stretch out between them. Her petulant tone reminded him of his sweet nieces when they were overtired and cranky.

"I know you *can*, but I'm enjoying touching you, and it would be rude to deny me the privilege after I stopped and pulled you out of the dust storm, don't you think?"

"Oh, you're good. I'll bet you can charm ladies out of their panties without breaking a sweat." For the first time, he heard a bit of amusement in her tone, and it warmed him to know she was relaxing enough to find her sense of humor.

"I'm scandalized by your presumption. I'll have you know my sisters consider me almost housebroken. They've spent years trying to civilize me, and despite their somewhat unorthodox and often painful teaching methods, they are proud of their success—although I will admit, they still consider me a work in progress."

He started combing at the bottom of her hair and slowly worked his way higher. The process was relatively painless since he'd been careful to finger comb the long strands several times while shampooing and conditioning.

"You have beautiful hair, *Cariña*. I'm looking forward to watching the firelight dance over the tapestry of color as it dries." *I'm also anxious to see what it looks like fanned out over my thighs as you suck me dry or the way the breeze lifts it when Trac and I fuck you outside under the stars.*

"Who's dancing in the firelight? Please tell me it's Lakyn, and she'll be naked. Beautiful. Naked. Woman. Firelight. A lot to love there," Trac's voice sounded from beside them. His friend's sudden appearance shouldn't have surprised Juan, but he'd become lost in the moment and hadn't checked the time.

"It's a good thing I'm used to my team's constant barrage of nonsense. I can snooze my way right through it."

Juan had noted Lakyn's calm acceptance of another person walking into the room when she was so scantily covered. Hell, this sort of thing was probably an everyday occurrence for her, no wonder she hadn't been surprised.

Juan loved displaying a submissive in public. There was something innately erotic about knowing others were admiring what he and Trac alone were allowed to touch. Most subs had at least a sliver of trepidation when came to being nude or partially exposed in public. That edge of vulnerability was something he loved to exploit, knowing it added a new dimension for most women.

Now that he thought about it, Juan realized that might be harder to achieve with Lakyn. From what he'd heard about models, modesty quickly became a thing of the past once their careers took off. With people surrounding them all the time—pulling one outfit off while others were fitting the next one in place, make-up artists and hair stylists applying touch-ups—it was a given any semblance of privacy was probably a pipedream.

"Probably a survival skill." Trac's response pulled Juan out of his wandering thoughts and back to the moment. Holding up a garment he'd been hiding behind his back, Trac held up a silk dress and grinned. "Mia said she'd brought you sweats, but since there's been a change in plans, I bought something better." Juan raised a brow in question, and Trac's grin told him the *change* was going to be something he'd like. "Kent and Kyle are setting up a private scene on one of the smaller stages."

Helping Lakyn to her feet, he watched as she turned to Trac, eyes widening at the dress hooked over his thick fingers. The garment looked more like a scrap of fabric than a dress, and Juan could hardly wait to see her wearing it. She shivered, the reaction making her entire body quake, and Juan wanted to pump his fist in the air.

"Where's the rest of it?" He suspected she'd tried to sound indignant, but the breathless quiver in her voice gave away her interest. Trac's predatory smile was all the answer she needed.

LAKYN WASN'T SURE how, but she knew this was a defining moment for her. She'd come to Texas for several reasons, and if she didn't take this opportunity, it might not come again. Her mind and body needed rest she wouldn't get unless she felt safe, and she wanted to learn more about the lifestyle she'd found herself inexplicably drawn to. If she'd learned one thing during her career, it was how quickly it could all be gone. A wrong word to someone at a party, a moment's inattention driving, it only took a heartbeat to change the rest of your life... or to end it. She didn't want to spend the rest of her life wondering what might have been.

When Trac didn't answer her question about the rest of the dress, she felt a surge of energy she wouldn't have thought possible. If you had asked her an hour ago, Lakyn would have sworn she'd depleted all her reserves, but now, she found herself coursing with a restless need to find out what was happening downstairs in the club. She reached for the dress, but Trac shook his head. Tilting her head to the side in confusion, she felt Juan's warm breath against her ear, "Arms up." Without taking time to wonder why her arms were raising, she'd put them over her head, slightly apart, waiting for Trac to slip the dress into place and gasped as the towel that had been wrapped securely around her pooled at her feet.

Cool air rushed over her bare skin, making her nipples tighten into stiff points. It was a natural instinct to drop her hands and cover her bare breasts, but she was surprised at the realization her wrists were shackled above her head by Trac's large hand. His free hand smoothed the silk he dropped over her naked torso. She was left with her arms stretched above her head, knowing the dress wasn't long enough to cover her pink bits.

"Fuck me, *Cariña*, you are so beautiful. I love the way the silk brushes over the globes of your ass." The appreciation in Juan's voice warmed her, but it didn't change the fact a stiff breeze was going to have her flashing everyone with a clear line of vision.

But who cares, I'm totally loving the way your fingertips are teasing those same well-rounded cheeks. Now, if you wouldn't mind just slipping those inquisitive digits just a little further south and... She barely held back her groan of frustration when Juan's fingers stopped their southern track and moved to her hip instead.

"Before we join the others, we need to make sure we're all on the same page, Lakyn." Trac's voice made her blink several times to refocus on what he was saying. Hell, when had she closed her eyes and leaned back against Juan? Crickets, she was going to have to pay attention if she was going to max-out this experience because she knew too well how quickly people tired of having celebrities around. It wasn't that she didn't understand why because she did. There was too much drama and not as many rewards as many believed.

She couldn't go out into public with being recognized, so something as simple as a girls' night out was impossible. Shopping trips? Guaranteed disaster. Dinner with friends? A leisurely walk through the park? None of those things were possible. Once she'd become successful, it hadn't taken long for most of her friends to move on because they'd realized what a pain in the ass it was to spend time with her. By her estimation, the people at Prairie Winds should last long enough for her to get in touch with Cooper, and once he was back stateside, it should be safe for her to go back to New York.

"I'm not sure what put that sad look in your eyes, dar- lin', but I want you to push it aside for a minute." Trac's deep voice washed over her, and she was more than happy to think about something else. "Tobi says you are interest- ed in learning about Dominance and submission, is that correct?" When she nodded, Trac's eyes seemed to flair with something she couldn't identify. "Juan and I would be happy to help."

"It would be our privilege to guide you. We're both experienced Dominants, and we're both interested in you, *Cariña*. I hope Tobi has sold you on ménage. Polyamorous relationships are very common at the Prairie Winds Club."

"I'm not going to lie, it seemed very odd at first, but Tobi did a great job of explaining how it works for her. I don't think there is a man in the world who would be interested in me long-term, let alone two, but I'd appreci- ate you taking me under your respective wings." She noted their frowns and wondered about what looked like an unspoken communication passing between them. She didn't ask because, in her experience, people rarely told you the unvarnished truth, and it was less painful to be uninformed than lied to.

"We're going to table this discussion until later because our friends are waiting for us, but rest assured, we'll be revisiting your comment about long-term interest."

The stern tone of Trac's voice surprised her. She had

no idea why he would be upset about her comment. She didn't take the distance people put between them personally—Lakyn understood how annoying the circus that surrounded her was.

Unlike many celebrities, she never complained about the isolation resulting from loss of friendships because she understood how unbelievably fortunate she'd been... she also knew success was fleeting, so she'd thrown herself headfirst into her career with single-minded focus. Lakyn Storm was known in the industry for her work ethic and for being easy to direct... a trait she attributed to having a bossy older brother. With a quick nod, she let them take her hands, but a few steps later she came to an abrupt halt.

"Wait. Shit, I forgot I need to finish dressing, and I'll need moisturizer and—" she didn't finish because her ass suddenly felt like it was on fire. It took her brain a few seconds to process the blow had come from Trac. Spinning on him, she glowered, "What the holy fucking hell? What was that for? I don't have on any damned underwear, my hair is straight as string, I need moisturizer because my face is a fucking business asset, and I don't go out in public without eyeliner and lip gloss... not ever." She was jamming her finger into his massive chest as fury raged through her.

"I've just spent days driving without stopping because I attract too much damn attention, I got fucking sandblasted on the edge of the road, picked up by a couple of guys who want to teach me about Dominance and submission, got snubbed by a woman I thought was my friend, and took a shower with a man I'd only known an hour. I'm pretty damned close to the edge, don't push me over, you won't like how it ends. Don't be fooled by the pretty face you see on screen and in magazines. I can be a real pain in the ass when provoked… just ask Cooper."

When she saw amusement in his eyes, Lakyn shook her head. "Laugh at me, and I swear I will shoot you with your own gun."

Chapter Five

J UAN STEPPED BETWEEN Lakyn and Trac before she had a complete melt-down. Trac was his best friend, but he wasn't big on compromise. Juan, on the other hand, had learned the fine art of finesse during his years living in a household surrounded by strong-willed women. There was a time to push and there was a time to soothe—and this was definitely the latter.

"*Cariña,* check in the bathroom for moisturizer, lip gloss, and any other cosmetic that will make you feel more at home. Your comfort is important to us, but you need to be quick about it. When you return, we'll join the others." When she started to speak, he shook his head. "No, precious, you are wearing exactly what we want you to wear. Your introduction to the lifestyle begins now." Her mouth snapped shut, and she glared at them as if that would solve her problem.

"She wants a spanking, that's what she's waiting for. For crying out loud, she talks like a dock worker. That language should *not* be a part of her vocabulary. Hell, she makes Tobi sound like a kindergarten teacher." Trac's barked words seemed to jolt her into action, and she turned on her heel and stomped back to the bathroom. Before she could fling the door closed, Trac growled, "Slam the door and you'll get the paddling you're angling for, Princess." Juan heard her muttering as the door closed silently and barely managed to hold back his grin at Trac's glower.

"Damn, brother, I think you may have met your match." Trac's size alone intimidated most submissives into behaving, but Lakyn had gone toe-to-toe with him, and it warmed Juan's heart to see his friend challenged. Trac might think he enjoyed complete submission and sweet compliance in his subs, but Juan had seen how quickly his friend lost interest in those women. Earning Lakyn's trust wasn't going to be easy, but he had a feeling it would be worth every ounce of effort.

"You're going to spoil her rotten, aren't you? There won't be a disciplined bone in her body when you're done. Protocol is going to fly out the window." Seeing Trac off-balance was something new, and Juan was enjoying it more than he should. Trac sighed and shook his head, "Fuck me, she is so beautiful, and I'm not just talking about the way she looks. There is a fire inside her that shines all the way to the surface."

"There are shadows, too. The loneliness lurking behind the bravado worries me. I hope she sticks around long enough for us to show her it's okay to let go and share those burdens." Lakyn's incredible transformation surprised Juan when she stepped out of the bathroom. She'd been gone five minutes, but she looked like she'd spent hours having her hair and makeup done.

"*Cariña*, I'm not sure I've ever known a woman who could get ready so quickly. I assure you my sisters cannot." She smiled as her cheeks turned a sweet shade of pink. It amazed him that a woman he knew was no stranger to compliments about her appearance would blush from his simple remark. Realizing he hadn't mentioned her beauty, but praised her efficiency gave him a bit more insight into the woman behind the pretty face.

"Let's go, our hosts are waiting." Trac's words might have sounded harsh to Lakyn, but Juan heard more than the rough edge of his friend's tone. Trac was aroused and fighting the urge to forgo the party for something a lot more intimate. His earlier threat to spank her had been more about his need to see her draped over his lap than about disciplining her.

Trac Hughes was well-known for his appreciation of the female derriere. He loved having the soft globes pressed into his large hands and claimed there was no better view of a woman's ass than when it was laid over his lap.

Juan hadn't fully understood the allure until they'd played with one of the club's submissives one night, and his friend had verbally walked him through it—step-by-step during their scene. The young woman they'd been playing with had orgasmed from Trac's words alone, and Juan had been enthralled as he briefly saw the world through the other man's eyes.

People were often surprised to learn Juan and Trac were friends because, on the surface, their personalities seemed polar opposite, but it was those differences that were their strength. They complimented each other professionally as well as in their personal lives. By the time they reached the club's main room, Lakyn's eyes were darting back and forth as if she was watching for someone.

"Who are you looking for, *Cariña?*" She startled at his direct question and when she looked up at him, Juan was surprised to see how truly anxious she'd become.

"I don't know why I thought I could do this. Fucking hell, this dress is going to disappear entirely with the first camera flash. I know better than this." When she started to turn, he wrapped his hand around her slender upper arm, stilling her retreat. Juan might have been the one to hold her, but it was Trac who stepped forward, blocking her view of the room. Gently lifting her chin with his fingers, Trac used every inch of his six-and-a-half-foot height to his advantage.

"Princess, no one is going to take your picture. There is a very strict no electronics rule at the club. Only a select few members are allowed to keep their phones on them—doctors, first responders, select members of the staff, and the club's owners. Anyone who has been given the privilege isn't going to risk a lifetime ban from not only this club but hundreds of others by taking a picture."

Juan had known she was tense, but he'd underestimated how close she'd been to the edge until Trac's words registered. She took a shuddering breath and finally began to relax. Trac smiled down at her and shook his head.

"Sorry, darlin' we should have mentioned that upstairs, but I have to admit, I'm looking forward to playing with the flash on my phone later to see if I really can make that dress disappear."

LAKYN COULDN'T HOLD back her giggle at the way Trac waggled his eyebrows when he'd told her how much he was looking forward to seeing if her dress would actually disappear under a flash. She could assure him it would indeed appear completely sheer. She'd made the mistake of wearing the wrong fabric to a gallery opening when she first started modeling. The pictures of her on the red carpet that night still lit up the internet now and then.

Her saving grace had been the panties she'd refused to

give up. Her stylist had been furious because she felt the panty lines ruined the look, but Lakyn had been adamant she wasn't going out in public without underwear. It was bad enough everyone had gotten an unobstructed view of her breasts. Not only had Lakyn been mortified by the pictures, her brother had gone completely thermonuclear. She'd known the minute he saw the photos because her phone had started ringing, non-stop.

Warm lips caressed her bare shoulder, startling her back to the moment.

"Stay with us, *Cariña*. Those lapses in attention will earn you a lot of paddlings, and I assure you, Master Trac is going to be happy to have you over his knee at the slightest provocation. I would suggest you make it your mission to ensure those spankings are for your pleasure rather than as punishment."

Juan's words sent a wave of heat through her, and she felt her pussy moisten. Good grief, how was she ever going to get through this without the evidence trailing down her thighs? What had she been thinking coming down here without panties? Oh, that's right, she hadn't been given a choice.

"Are you planning to join us, or is Juan going to eat her alive in the hallway?" Lakyn jumped at the sound of a deep voice to her right. "Easy, sweetness, I didn't mean to startle you." She recognized Kent West and gave him a quick smile. "Come on, we're going to do a demo with some of the new merchandise from the Forum Shops. We're calling it an etiquette lesson for our sweet sub. That sounds a lot nicer than punishment, don't you think?"

Lakyn didn't respond because she assumed the question had been rhetorical. When all three men paused and turned their attention to her, she took a quick step back.

"Freeze." Trac's command had the desired effect, and she went completely still. "I know you aren't familiar with the rules yet, Princess, but when a Dom or Mistress asks you a question, they expect an answer. This isn't the social scene you are used to, there is no pretense. You'll find a lot of freedom in that, once you discover it's real."

She might not know him well, but she understood the sharp edge she heard in Trac's voice. This was a man who had an intimate knowledge of the subtle nuances of polite society's undercurrents of communication, and she'd be willing to bet he hated it. *Interesting.*

Nodding her understanding, she turned her attention to Kent, she could play this game. Hell, she'd practically elevated it to an Olympic sport.

"Yes, Mr. West, I agree, the semantics of lessons are much nicer than less than subtle nuances of punishment although I don't believe you felt any real need for my approval. I just remembered I promised to meet Mia upstairs. She was going to make me something to eat. It would be rude to leave her in a lurch." His eyes widened in surprise a split second before he leaned his head back and laughed. When he finally regained a measure of decorum, his eyes were still dancing with amusement.

"Damn, I'm not sure I've ever been told off that sweetly since the last time I accidentally stumbled into one of my mother's hen parties."

"Of course, referring to it as a hen party had nothing to do with the fact they cut you off at the knees without breaking a sweat." Kyle West's southern drawl filled the air as he stepped around his brother, taking in the group with a quick look around. "I'm not sure what you said to my brother to remind him of that humbling experience, but I'd like to thank you just the same. It always does my heart good to see my little brother brought to heel although you might want to be careful about this particular venue." This time it was Lakyn's turn to laugh. She recognized a smackdown when she heard one, no matter how veiled. Kyle West had just warned her to watch her mouth inside the club. *Message received.*

"True on all counts. Never let it be said southern women can't take you down a peg or two, and we all know sugar doesn't hold a candle to their sweetness while they're doing it. I assure you, I was much more respectful to the lovely ladies of the Rose Society after that *unfortunate incident.*" The way Kent said the last two words told Lakyn he'd been quoting someone, she suspected his mother, and it was all she could do to hold back her smile.

Without further comment, they all moved to a small stage area, and Lakyn was surprised to see so many people gathered in the small space. There was no way they'd all be able to sit in the lounge chairs and sofas scattered around the area in front of the stage.

The tall plants bordering the enclosure made it seem intimate without walls, and Lakyn wondered who had designed the club's interior. There were obvious nods to the old west, but it was clear the designer hadn't felt the need to turn it into a western movie set. The sleek lines of the lighting over the stage hid the riggings Tobi had told her about, and Lakyn leaned down trying to get a better look at the elaborate array of steel cables and pulleys.

"Come." Trac grasped her hand in his much larger one and moved to the side, so they'd be closer to the stage. "You seem very interested in how things work, so we'll stand here. It will give you a clearer view, and there is always the added bonus of having you on your feet." When she looked up and him in confusion, his answering grin made him look more like an ornery teen than a former soldier. Juan had given her a brief overview of their backgrounds while he'd been combing the tangles from her hair, and she'd had to admit, the information had gone a long way to convince her she was safe in their care.

Juan leaned close to whisper, "We plan to monitor your responses very carefully during the scene, *Cariña*. Since Tobi's Masters are going to use a variety of new toys on her, we'll get a chance to find out what you find appealing."

"So, it's okay for me to talk? I thought Kyle's words sounded like a warning. I am worried about Mia, she was so nice to offer to feed me."

"No, it's isn't okay for you to speak unless you're given permission or asked a direct question. Remember, you address Doms as Master Kent, Master Kyle, Mistress Rebecca, Sir, or Madame will also work. Mia knows the plan changed. There is food across the room, and we'll make sure you eat when you're hungry." Trac paused for a heartbeat, but it was long enough for her to wonder what he was planning to say he thought she wasn't going to appreciate. "We are the only Doms you will address simply as Master."

"That's because you belong to us, and we belong to you." She'd understood what Trac had been trying to say since this was a point made in almost all the erotic novels she'd read, but she felt her cheeks flush with Juan's blatant admission. "We'll also settle for Sir—for now." She felt herself tremble as the heat from her cheeks spread over her exposed skin.

"I love seeing that flush of arousal, Princess. Come

here." He held out his hand, and when she slid her palm against his, Trac pulled her roughly against his chest. "You're just a little bit, baby. I'm going to have to get you a stepstool, so I can kiss you for as long as I like without breaking my back." Before his words worked their way through her desire fogged mind, he'd cradled the back of her head in his enormous palm and bent her slowly backward until her back was arched, her tightly peaked nipples pressed firmly against his chest. The first touch of his lips against hers sent tiny pinpricks of heat through her brain, and he took full advantage of her gasp.

The kiss was scorching hot, Trac's tongue plunging deep and sweeping the inside of her mouth. He tasted sweet and smelled like citrus mint. When she sighed against his lips, he pulled her tighter against him. There was no mistaking the steel of his erection searing against her, and she found herself wiggling against his length in an effort to elicit some kind of response. A stinging swat against her almost bare ass made her jerk in his arms. He pulled back enough to speak.

"You're playing with fire, Princess," he growled. "Don't think we won't waltz you out of here and fuck you on the nearest horizontal surface." The sexual tension between them was practically crackling in the air.

Kyle's voice sounded over the speakers, breaking the mood, and Lakyn wasn't sure if she was grateful for the chance to clear her head or disappointed for the lost moment. She tried to listen to what Kyle West was saying, but his words faded into the background quickly as she watched Kent securing their wife inside a large polished steel circle.

"You'll notice this ring is new. Since Tobi and several

of the other submissives in the club are petite, we commissioned this. It's a new and much-improved version of the one suspended above." When Kyle's words finally made their way through the haze of Lakyn's arousal, she looked up to see a larger ring suspended in the rigging above the stage.

"As usual, Clint and the creative crew at E.G.A. Fabrication in Sealy have exceeded our expectations. We'll be having a separate demonstration tomorrow night to show you the added safety features and the numerous modifications designed with your pleasure in mind. I'm confident you'll be as pleased as I am with the changes." Kyle continued to speak about the hinges and torso straps, but Lakyn's focus locked on the interplay between Kent and Tobi.

Kent's hands rarely left her for more than a second or two as he secured the straps around her wrists, ankles, and torso. Next, he threaded a long piece of silk through a small metal loop on the inside of the ring. Tying it off, he pulled the silk behind Tobi's head. Before he wrapped it all the way around her head, he pressed soft kisses over each of her eyes, and even though Lakyn couldn't hear what he was saying, it was easy to see Tobi visibly relax as he spoke. After securing the end of the silk cloth to loop on the opposite side of the ring, Kent carefully fanned the fabric out over the back of her blonde hair and tucked her long blonde braid securely between the folds.

The dress Tobi wore was what the fashion houses call an exaggerated A-line halter, but Lakyn had always thought of the simple design as a tent dress. With her arms extended to the eleven and one o'clock positions on the ring, the audience was being treated to a teasing view of her very bare pussy lips. Unless you were looking closely, you might not notice the dark rose colored petals, but Lakyn took in every nuance of the picture in front of her, and it was the single most erotic thing she'd ever seen.

Chapter Six

JUAN WATCHED AS Lakyn stood stock still, totally enthralled with the Wests' scene. She'd completely forgotten about eating, and he made a mental note to watch that carefully. Her responses were so open, and with her guard down, he was amazed to see how much younger she looked. Lakyn Hicks craved everything she was seeing play out on stage—or at least her body did. Opening up the world of kink for her would be a joy; the only problem would be breaching the walls Lakyn Storm had carefully erected to protect herself from the challenges inherent to her career.

"Tell me what you see, *Cariña*." He knew she would unconsciously prioritize what she was watching, and if she was honest with herself and them, she'd describe the most personally significant things first. He was surprised when she only hesitated briefly before speaking.

"The silk covering Tobi's eyes is so finely woven, she must feel like she's wrapped in a cloud. And the way Kent fanned out the fabric at the back of her head like a miniature hammock tells me they're being very careful her neck is protected, no matter how far back she is tilted." How fitting that a model would zero in on the silk scarf; he had to fight back his amusement, so he didn't distract her. "Her dress is an interesting style, and I wonder how many people have noticed her bare labia peeking out from beneath the folds of the dress. Tobi mentioned she is self-conscious of the stretch marks on her breasts, and I wonder if they'll wait until the lights are dimmed before they bare her completely."

"Princess, you're absolutely right. Both of her Doms are acutely aware of what she considers flaws, but they consider those marks proof of the precious gifts she's given them. The only thing Kent and Kyle West love more than their children is the woman who lights up their lives in every way. One of most appealing aspects of the lifestyle is the intensity of the connection between Doms and their submissives."

"Tobi said the same thing. She explained it was, in large part, due to the emphasis on communication." For a moment she wondered if it was rude to be talking to Juan and Trac without looking at them, but she couldn't take her eyes off what was happening on the stage. Kent had tilted the ring back far enough to put Tobi off-balance. Lakyn noted the other woman hadn't jumped or reacted in any of the ways you'd expect of someone who'd been moved to the tipping point. *What would it be like to have that level of trust in someone?*

"Tell me what you're thinking, Princess. Your entire body shuddered, and I want to know why."

There was an edge to Trac's voice she hadn't heard before, and she found herself responding without taking time to filter her words. It wasn't easy to put the jumble of thoughts that had run through her head into words, but she did the best she could. When she'd finished, he pressed a kiss to the sensitive spot behind her ear.

"Well done, little sub. You picked out one of the most important elements of any D/s relationship. First and foremost, submission is always the submissive's choice—

you hold all the power, contrary to how it may appear. Tobi could stop this scene any time she wanted with the utterance of a single word."

"Her Masters trust her to tell them if it's too much. Tobi's honesty and transparency are the basis for their trust. It may appear seamless now, but I can assure you, polyamorous relationships require a unique level of all of these elements, and the Wests fought hard to get to this point."

Juan's admiration for his friends was easy to hear, and she found herself nodding her understanding. Tobi had been very forthcoming during their conversations, and Lakyn appreciated the other woman's candor. Without that background, she'd be more overwhelmed than aroused by what she was watching now.

Kyle exchanged the handheld microphone for a wireless clip-on he hadn't switched on yet. Lakyn watched with a mix of wonder and envy as he leaned close to Tobi's ear. The audience couldn't hear what he was saying, but it wasn't difficult to see Tobi's reaction. Her eyes went impossibly wide, and she slowly nodded.

"Kyle won't let her get away with not speaking her answer. Watch." Juan's words were prophetic because Kyle immediately shook his head and pulled back. His intensity was so forceful, Lakyn would have sworn she could feel it from where she stood along the wall.

She studied Tobi as the other woman answered whatever questions her Masters asked. Her body was practically vibrating with desire, and Lakyn felt the anxiety she'd felt at Tobi's earlier greeting begin to melt away. Mia's reassurances about Tobi's sincerity replayed in her mind as she watched the pretty blonde relax even further into the bindings. Kent uncovered a tray before rolling it closer.

The first item he picked up caused a ripple of surprise to move through the crowd. As soon as he slipped the headphones over Tobi's ears, Kyle switched on the mic clipped to his shirt.

"Our lovely sub is very good at picking up the smallest verbal clues from audiences, these noise-canceling head-phones will keep her from hearing you or our commentary." A grin curved the corners of his mouth, and Lakyn suspected she'd just seen a glimpse of the ornery boy he had no doubt been.

"Unless we want her to be included—then it's as simple as tapping a button on our lapel mics." Lakyn noticed Kent's tone was harsher now that he wasn't speaking to his wife. Rather than being put off by the change, Lakyn found herself admiring the difference. It was an outward sign of his devotion and loyalty, two of the things she admired the most. Lakyn had seen enough infidelity among her co-workers and acquaintances to last a lifetime.

Kyle explained they were adding several sets of the headphones to the club's equipment inventory and a few mics for demos, prompting cheers from most of the on-lookers. Lakyn was mesmerized by what she was seeing, but she tuned out what the men were saying when it became clear they'd meant it when they'd said this would be a demo. *I understand they are using this to enlighten their members about new products, but it sounds like a late-night infomercial to me. Okay, a really hot, kinky informercial, but still...*

JUAN STUDIED LAKYN'S ever-changing expressions as she watched the scene. It didn't appear as though she was listening to what Kyle was saying, but she seemed completely enraptured by what she was seeing. Her eyes were so dilated, there was only a narrow ring of color showing, and the pulse at the base of her neck was pounding so rapidly, he could barely track the beats. He listened as her respiration accelerated and frowned when he noted she was intermittently holding her breath.

From the look Trac gave him over Lakyn's shoulder, he hadn't missed the hitches in her breathing either. Juan watched the muscles in his friend's arms tighten around her shoulders as a subtle reminder for her to take a breath.

"What do you see now, *Cariña?*" Years of experience had taught Juan to let submissives describe what they were seeing—it was like taking a walk through their minds. As long as she answered honestly, it would give them a good idea of what she found most arousing.

"They've taken away her ability to move... she can only hear what they allow, and the silk scarf they tied over her eyes deprives her of the chance to anticipate anything. She can only feel. I remember her telling me the more restrictive the scene, the more freedom it gave her. I didn't understand at the time, but now it's so easy to see. Tobi doesn't have to wonder if she is being too aggressive or if she's not showing enough interest. She doesn't have to worry about splitting her time fairly between her two Doms because they're in control of everything." Lakyn's voice sounded almost wistful and Juan was thrilled with her observations.

"*Cariña,* can you see yourself in those bonds? Can you imagine putting yourself in our care, trusting us with your pleasure?" She finally turned her face toward his and the depth of her desire shone so brightly in her eyes it stole his breath.

"Yes, I want to know what if feels like to lose myself in pleasure. I want to let someone else make decisions for a little while." From what little Juan had learned about her alter-ego, Lakyn Storm only had two people in her life to share the burden—a manager who didn't appear to be particularly committed to looking out for her best interests and a brother who loved and protected her but was rarely available. One of the things Juan's sisters had taught him was the importance of what they called *being present*. It had taken him a long time to figure out exactly what they'd been talking about.

Teaching him how to actively listen was one of the greatest gifts his sisters had ever given him. They'd also drilled into him the importance of touch. They still re-minded him anytime he was within arm's reach about the healing power of a hug.

Trac leaned down, whispering in her ear, "If I slide my fingers between your lovely legs will I find you wet for us, Princess?" Juan was grateful his friend had picked up the ball while he'd been lost in thought. This was one of the reasons he enjoyed ménage. It was also one of the many reasons he believed a polyamorous marriage was the way to go.

"Yes." Her breathless response would have made Juan's cock rock hard even if it hadn't already been pressing incessantly against his zipper.

Juan moved to stand in front of her and gave her nip-ples a gentle pinch. "Try again, *Cariña.*"

"Yes, Sir, you will find me drenched." The conviction in her voice was far more convincing than the single word response she'd given them the first time.

As much as Juan wished they could whisk her away, it was better to play at the club—at least this first time. It was important for those new to the lifestyle to have the security of people nearby until they had time to establish trust. Making love to her in the privacy of their cabin was one thing, tying her to the bed and fucking her until none of them could move was another.

TRAC SLIPPED HIS hand under her dress and growled against her ear, "Open for me" when he found her legs locked together. He suspected she was trying to keep the proof of her arousal from running in tempting rivulets down the inside of her thighs, but he could tell her it was wasted effort. She'd soon learn what a turn on it was for a Dom to see the wanton evidence of his or her effect on a submissive. When he felt her head turn quickly from side to side, he tightened his left arm around her upper torso.

"It's not your job to worry about who is watching, Princess. If Master Juan or I want to show off what belongs to us, that's for us to decide. All you need to worry about is following instructions and trusting us to give you exactly what you need." Her legs slid apart, the response so immediate, he groaned in appreciation. Damn, the woman ignited something deep inside him he hadn't even known existed.

All Trac could think about was possessing the woman in his arms. She was a natural submissive, her responses had been forthright, and she admitted her interest in learning more about the lifestyle that was a huge part of his life. Trac had known he needed to be in charge in bedroom long before he knew there was a term for it. Learning there was a lifestyle centered around what felt like a part of his very soul had been a life-changing moment.

Looking down at Lakyn, he felt like he was fast approaching another huge fork in life's road. The path he chose would determine where life led, and he was anxious to get started. Finding Lakyn on the side of the road had been a fluke, but her agreement to let them teach her about Dominance and submission was a gift he planned to fully appreciate. For the first time in years, Trac was beginning to rethink his aversion to commitment.

"Is she slick?" Juan's question jolted him back to the moment, and he held up his fingers for his friend to see the shining evidence coating his fingers. "Christ, all that glistening honey is going to push me right over the damned edge of sanity." Taking a small step back, so he had a clearer view of her, Juan crossed his arms over his broad chest and smiled.

"Make her come. I want to see what she looks like when her mind shatters from pleasure." Her eyes must have gone wide with fear because Juan quickly shook his head. "Don't worry about anything but giving yourself over to the pleasure Master Trac is going to bring you, *Cariña*."

He wouldn't tell her he had no intention of letting anyone hear the sweet sounds of her pleasure. It wasn't that he was a prude, hell he loved public play as much as the next Dom, but this was the Wests' scene, and he wasn't about to upstage them. Juan looked on as Lakyn's eyes closed, and her soft moan was echoed by Trac.

"Princess, you're so hot and wet. You might as well throw away every pair of panties you own because I want to be able to touch you just like this anytime the urge strikes me. Feeling the soft petals of your pussy lips slipping between my fingers is hotter than hell."

Juan stepped closer, so he'd be ready to seal his mouth over hers when the orgasm building like a tsunami finally swamped her. Lakyn was vibrating with energy, and the pink flush of arousal spreading over her upper chest let him know she was close to falling over the edge. Juan watched as Lakyn's mouth opened and quickly closed the space between them, slanting his mouth over hers, capturing her cries of release. She fisted the sides of his shirt in her small hands as if it was a lifeline tethering her to Earth. He ended the kiss when he saw her sag in Trac's arms.

"You are beautiful when you come, *Cariña,* and I can't wait to feel all of that passion when we're in a much more intimate place."

"Your pussy is so tight, Princess, we're going to need to be very careful with you." Trac's words sent a deep flush over Lakyn's cheeks, making Juan wonder how long it had been since she'd been intimate with a man. When his friend withdrew his hand from beneath her dress and sucked a single finger into this mouth to savor the taste of her essence, Juan felt his eyes widen with concern.

One finger? Trac's comment took on a whole new level of significance when Juan realized his friend had only used a single digit to penetrate her. Hell, they were going to need to be extremely careful because both he and Trac were larger than average, and the last thing he wanted to do was hurt her. He'd seen what could happen when an inexperienced sub wasn't properly prepared for a Dom's cock, and it wasn't pretty.

"Holy shit, I can't believe I just came in the middle of a room filled with strangers." Lakyn's breathless confession might have been amusing if it hadn't contained profanity.

Juan watched Trac's expression turn thunderous. Before he could blink, Lakyn's eyes went wide and she yelped as Trac's massive palm smacked her ass.

"Language, Princess. You'll speak respectfully or not at all." Juan almost laughed out loud at the easy-to-read expression on Lakyn's face. Trac wasn't going to be able to pry a word from her with a crowbar. *I do believe my stubborn friend has just met his match.* "Do you understand?"

Trac's question was met with stubborn silence as Lakyn crossed her arms over her chest in defiance. Juan wanted to avoid interrupting the Wests' scene any more than they already had and gave Trac a quick nod to the nearest exit. They needed to move this discussion outside the small scene area. His friend was clearly frustrated, but Lakyn looked like her head was about to spin around on her shoulders powered by the steam he could practically see coming out of her ears.

Juan wanted to shake his head because this was going to be a battle neither of them would win. Just as he had so many times with his sisters, Juan was going to be forced to act as the referee. Fucking hell, this is not how he'd seen the rest of their evening playing out. Leading the two of them through a back door leading to a secluded terrace sheltered from the thunderstorm raging a few feet away, he opened his mouth to speak, but the little tiger rounded on Trac before he got out a single word of warning.

"What the hell is wrong with you whacking on me like I'm an errant child? Good grief, didn't your mother teach you any damned manners? God bless a goose, you can't go around swatting people just because you don't like what they have to say. Haven't you ever heard of the First Amendment? Good fucking Lord, I can't believe it. My language isn't that bad, I'm a damned saint compared to most of the people I know. Hell, even my brother doesn't bitch about my language, and his pucker factor is off the fucking chart about almost everything related to me."

If he hadn't been so shocked by her tirade, Juan might have been able to enjoy the fact Trac was utterly speechless. He'd never known his best friend to be completely flummoxed by a sub. *I'm not sure I've ever seen that particular shade of purple on another human's face before.* Lakyn was poking her finger into Trac's chest, emphasizing her words with short jabs with her French-tipped nails, and he almost lost control of the laughter he'd been valiantly holding back when Trac flinched.

"What? You don't have anything to say? Boy oh boy, I can't fucking believe you. All pissy because of a curse word and now the damned cats got your tongue. Well, believe you me, I'm a New Yorker now, and we can dress you down seven ways to Sunday and never break a sweat. You can just suck it up, buster, because big girls know bad words too." She turned on her heel and started pacing the width of the patio, muttering under her breath about the class Uncle Sam obviously taught military recruits where the newbie soldiers were brainwashed into believing they were the kings of all they surveyed.

When Trac started to reach for her, Juan laid his hand on his friend's forearm and shook his head.

"Let her wind down. This isn't really about you. She's crashing. Whatever she's running from back east, fatigue, hunger, her car petering out on her, the storm, and a mind shattering orgasm, the swat was the last straw and she's reeling. Just be ready to catch her." He'd no sooner uttered the last words when she seemed to trip over thin air and before she could right herself, Juan watched her eyes roll back, and she began free-falling. She'd have face planted if

Trac hadn't been already moving in her direction.

"Jesus, that was close. I swear I was ready to paddle her ass for that outburst. Hell, I'm still going to paddle her, but at least now I know it wasn't all disrespect." Juan pulled one of the soft subbie blankets from a nearby cabinet and wrapped it around her as she lay cradled in Trac's arms.

"I'll go get one of the golf carts. We need to take her to our place and get her settled. Those dark bruises under her eyes tell me she'll probably sleep for hours, and I'd rather she slept between us." Trac simply nodded his head, but as Juan turned to go, his friend finally found his voice.

"Thanks for keeping me from making a big mistake with her. I was so shocked, I forgot she is completely inexperienced. I don't care about what she's read or how much Tobi's told her, it's completely different when you come face to face with D/s for the first time." Juan nodded and felt a wave of relief sweep over him knowing Trac had seen the bigger picture. His best friend finally chuckled as he brushed a stray lock of her hair from her cheek.

"I'll bet she gives Cooper a run for his money, and from what I remember, he was no pushover. Seeing them go toe-to-toe is probably worth the price of admission."

Yeah, probably a lot like what I what I watched play out a few minutes ago, but her brother probably isn't stunned into silence.

Chapter Seven

LAKYN TRIED TO surface through the fog of sleep, but she was so hot, all she could think about was escaping the tangle of blankets suffocating her. Before her mind could register where she was, a strong arm encircled her, and she was launched over the edge into a full-blown panic attack. Fighting as if her life depended on it, Lakyn's mind turned off, and all her brother's self-defense training kicked in. She heard soft grunts from the man trying unsuccessfully to pin her to the bed, but she wasn't going to stop fighting just because she thought she'd hurt him.

"*Cariña. Stop now!*" Something in the man's deep voice stilled the raging in her soul, and Lakyn froze. Sucking in deep breaths, she tried to search the darkness for a clue to where she was. Damn it, she couldn't see *anything*, she'd never had good night vision… it was one of the reasons she'd always slept with a small lamp on. Her breathing was starting to accelerate again as panic began edging back over her when she felt the bed shift, and with a nearly silent click, the room was illuminated in a soft glow.

Finally, able to get her bearings, it all came flooding back. Texas. Prairie Winds. Juan and Trac. She was safe. The man who'd tried to break into her apartment one night hadn't finally figured out a way past the security system Cooper had insisted she install. Pulling in huge gulps of air, Lakyn realized she was shaking as strong arms wrapped around her.

"*Cariña,* are you alright?"

Beside them, Trac groaned, "I'm the one you should be worried about. Fuck me, Princess, whoever taught you those moves should be damned proud. But I'm warning you right now, if I end up with a shiner and am subjected to a bunch of trash talk from my teammates, I'm paddling your ass." Trac's tone was petulant rather than threatening. Lakyn felt a giggle bubble to the surface and didn't even try to hold it back.

"So, it's okay for you to curse, but not me? How is that fair?" Her challenge might have carried more weight if she hadn't been snickering, but she doubted it.

"Princess, we have never made any claim about being fair. As Doms, we promise to give you what you need, and trust me—fair will never be a part of *that equation.*" The wicked gleam in his eyes as he rubbed his abused nose sent a shiver up her spine.

"Tell us what happened to send you into such a panic, *Cariña.*" Without releasing her, Juan pulled her on to his lap, sucking in a quick breath when her bare hip pressed against his equally bare erection. She was getting ready to wiggle against him, but he must have sensed her intent because he growled against her ear, "Don't. Tempting me when we are both naked and already in bed would end this discussion before it ever started, and I want you to answer my question."

Lakyn nodded and took a deep breath while she decided how much to share.

"I know that look, Princess, and I assure you, editing your response is lying by omission. I would imagine that came up a time or two during your chats with Tobi because I know she's been over the spanking bench at the club more than once for the same offense."

Trac was right, Tobi had mentioned the definition of lying was what she'd called 'broader than a damned barn' whatever that meant. Lakyn had assumed it meant there was more to lying than simply repeating facts inaccurately. It hadn't occurred to her keeping some of the uglier aspects of her fears to herself would be considered deception. *Fucking hell. I'm screwed. Might as well get this over with.* Nodding her understanding, she watched as Trac's brows drew together in a frown.

"Words, Lakyn. Use your damned words to answer questions. As my granny always said, 'I can't hear your head rattle, you know.'" She giggled at his attempt to imitate his grandmother's voice and wondered if the elderly woman knew her grandson quoted her.

"Yes, Sir, I understand, but I want you to know the whole story is pretty long, so I'm going to give you the abbreviated version now. We can revisit this discussion in the morning. Now that I've cooled off, I'm starting to get sleepy again. That was what woke me up, I was hot. I'm not used to sleeping with anyone and… well, you two are hot… in more ways than one."

The grins both men flashed her made them look more like the carefree young men she used to meet at public relations events when she'd first started modeling rather than the experienced Dominants she knew they were. Shaking her head to clear the errant thoughts, Lakyn shrugged her shoulders.

"I've been dealing with a stalker. Well, I guess you'd call him a stalker. Hell, I probably shouldn't assume it's a man. That's probably against some PC edict or some-thing." Shaking her head again at her own distraction, Lakyn took a deep breath, trying to re-focus her attention on the topic. "It started out innocent enough, but then they always do."

"You mean this has happened before?" Trac's question didn't surprise her, but the anger in his tone made her flinch even though she was sure his frustration wasn't directed at her.

"In my business, it happens all the time. Ordinarily, it's a minor inconvenience for a few weeks, then the 'admirer' finds a new, more worthy recipient of their affections. I've even had them send me fuck off letters, letting me know they were moving on because I'd failed to respond or in some other way I hadn't lived up to their expectations."

"*Cariña*, I'm not even sure what to say about this. It always baffles me how cruel people can be to those they claim to love or even those they previously cared about."

She smiled at Juan and tried to imagine what it would be like to have a line of defense between herself and the world. Cooper did all he could, but more often than not, he was on the other side of the world when things went wrong. She took another cleansing breath, wanting to get back on task before the rest of the night slipped between her fingers, and she was left feeling exhausted again tomorrow.

"This time, it felt different. I can't really explain why… maybe it's because I haven't been able to get in touch with Cooper." She shrugged but didn't think they'd been fooled by the nonchalant gesture.

"Probably instinct and that's not something you should ever ignore, *Cariña*."

Juan's hand slipped over hers, unfolding the fingers she'd unconsciously clenched as the stress of the past few months returned. Damn, sitting naked between two equally bare hunks had definitely distracted her from the reality of why she'd fled in New York.

Will they believe me or accuse me of having an over-active imagination like everyone back east?

"I KNOW, BUT it was hard to remember when everyone around me kept insisting I was over-reacting. One detective actually insinuated I was making everything up for publicity which was absurd since I was the one who insisted everything be kept out of the press."

Trac felt a surge of anger move through him but thankfully, before he could respond, she shook her head and muttered, "I'm sure Tobi was right, the asshat probably has a little dick." Trac didn't even try to hold back his laughter. God love Tobi, she'd broken the tension in the room without even being present.

"Princess, I don't even want to think about the size of another man's junk, but I'll look forward to chatting with him about how to show proper respect to my woman." Her eyes widened when he referred to her as his, but he didn't care. Juan's knowing smirk made Trac want to roll his eyes, but he held his immature responses in check. *Fucker is going to gloat about this forever.*

Juan smoothed the back of his hand down the side of Lakyn's face, and Trac watched Lakyn's reaction to the affectionate gesture. He'd always admired Juan's ability to soothe women with simple touches.

"I know you're tired but give us a quick overview of the problems you were having. We'll have Micah pull all the police reports, but from the sound of it, I'm not betting they'll provide much detail." Lakyn looked oddly relieved, and it didn't take long to figure out why.

"I can't tell you how much I appreciate that you believe me. My manager has an apartment in the same building where I live, and he insisted no one could get by the front desk security officer, but I know that's not true. Hell, I've walked in many times while the older man at the desk was busy without him seeing me slip past."

"Did they check the security cameras?" Trac couldn't imagine it being something the detective would forget, but if he didn't believe Lakyn was telling the truth, he might not have bothered.

"I asked them, but I'm not sure they did. Of course, by the time I settled down enough to ask the security staff about it myself, the tapes had looped and erased everything from the date of the first attempted break-in."

"First attempt? How many times did this happen?" Trac struggled to keep his anger in check. If they hadn't already put out a call to her brother, he'd damned well be doing it now.

"I'm not sure how many times they tried, but someone got in on three occasions, and yes, I'm certain about that number. I always secured strings and transparent tape over the door. I also had the locks changed regularly, and no, I never used the same locksmith twice." Trac had to admit, he was impressed. It was obvious from Juan's expression he also admired her moxie.

"Did your intruder take anything, *Cariña?*"

"He took clothing… things I'd worn. It's very creepy having someone in your space when you aren't there, but it's even worse when they steal panties out of your dirty clothes hamper." Having your personal space invaded would make anyone feel vulnerable, but having your intimate clothing stolen would add a whole other dimension to the feeling of violation. A shudder moved through her before she took a deep breath and attempted to smile.

"I guess I should be glad he didn't take the clean stuff." Her attempt at humor didn't come close to covering up her discomfort, but Trac wasn't going to call her out on it. It was obvious she needed to feel some measure of control in this situation. "Someone also tried to access the safe in my bedroom closet, but they weren't able to open it.

"The final straw was when a black SUV followed me down the street late one evening. I first noticed it as I walked to a nearby diner to eat, then on my way back to my apartment I saw the same car following me. I knew it was the same vehicle because the tag number was the same. The driver tried to cut me off at the corner outside my building, but I managed to pull myself free when a masked man opened one of the back doors and tried to pull me into the backseat."

"Did you notify the authorities?" Trac bet he already knew the answer, and honestly, he couldn't fault her when she shook her head indicating she hadn't bothered.

"It seemed pointless and would have only delayed my escape." She detailed how she'd packed and called two different cab companies, setting up a relay that would double back before dropping her off at a car rental agency a few blocks from her apartment. When they'd looked surprised, she'd shrugged. "They probably wouldn't have expected me to go to all that trouble, then return so close to home. I was trying to do the unexpected."

Trac was damned impressed, she'd taken great precautions, but then she'd made a huge error. "Why did you rent the car in your real name?"

"I didn't want to, but the jerk said I had to use the name on my driver's license, or he wouldn't let me have the car I'd already paid for. He wouldn't return my money either, the pissant. So, I drove as far as I could without stopping, hoping to elude them... and well, you know the rest of the story." He had a sinking feeling Lakyn had left out a lot, but she was fading fast and needed to rest. They'd have plenty of time to get the additional details tomorrow.

Juan excused himself to the restroom, and Trac was relieved to see him grab his cell off the nightstand. His friend would give the team the added information and get them started pulling the police reports. The attempted abduction upped their concern, and they needed to find out who'd added the tracking device to her rental when it appeared she'd done a good job of concealing what agency she planned to use. Micah had detected multiple trackers as soon as they'd driven through the front gate, so he'd sent someone out to check the car before it was towed.

Pulling her against his chest, Trac rubbed circles over her back until he felt her relax and her breathing even out. He wondered how much Lakyn knew about who her older brother actually worked for. His gut told him Cooper Hicks had deliberately kept his kid sister in the dark, hoping what she didn't know wouldn't hurt her. From what the West brothers had shared, they'd been trying to recruit Cooper for months, and the last they'd heard, he wanted to finish up his latest mission before coming to Texas to speak with Kent and Kyle personally.

Neither he nor Juan would tell Lakyn her brother was a CIA operative unless it became necessary, but something about the black SUV made the hair on the back of his neck stand straight up. He didn't know what Hicks was working on, but if someone was trying to manipulate him, picking up his sister in a snatch-and-grab would be damned effective. The flip side—Lakyn wasn't a large woman and wouldn't have been able to fight off a professional, making him think the attempted kidnapping hadn't been ordered by anyone with the resources to do it right. Before drifting off to sleep, Trac briefly wondered what was taking Juan so long, but the contentment of holding Lakyn in his arms quickly pulled him back into sleep.

COOPER HICKS SLIPPED back several steps, disappearing into the darkened alley thanks to his black clothing and grease-painted face. Cursing under his breath, he pulled his vibrating phone from his pocket and activate the darkened screen. The damned thing had been vibrating since he'd landed at Heathrow two hours ago, but he'd been hard pressed to get into position and hadn't taken the time to check it.

Hell, the thing lit up like a fucking Christmas tree before he could even get off the damned plane. The first full-court press of messages had been from his handler, informing him of the change to his mission. The change from apprehension to a simple photograph was a welcome relief. Photographing the man half the countries in the world were looking for was far easier than collaring the elusive arms dealer without back-up.

Half of those tracking the target wanted to strike a deal, the other half wanted to take him out of business. The change in his objective made him wonder if Uncle Sam hadn't flipped from one half to the other. Ordinarily, Cooper would be concerned about the strange things happening within the Agency, but he'd already made up his mind and would be leaving as soon as he returned state-side.

His handler and several others up the chain of command were doing everything in their respective powers to keep him on-board, but he was done. He'd hit a wall a few months ago, and in this business—burnout was a death sentence. It would take him at least a month to finish up paperwork and debrief, but once he was formally released from service, he'd be free and wouldn't answer to the United States government for the first time since he'd become an adult.

Cooper had cleared all the encoded messages, but it had evidently taken his phone longer to download the messages from regular phone carriers and the internet. Scrolling quickly through the list he felt his heart clench at the number of messages from Lakyn, her manager, and Kyle West. Most of the messages were long enough, he knew he'd have to wait until he returned to his hotel to sort through them, but Kyle's last message was the one that caught his eye.

We have L. Will keep her safe. Call ASAP.

How the hell had his little sister ended up in fucking Texas with the men who'd been trying to recruit him for months? Lakyn's ability to walk through a shit storm and come out smelling like a rose never ceased to amaze him. Shaking his head, Cooper slipped the phone back into his pocket and stepped silently out of the alley just in time to see a black Towne car approach. With a little luck, he'd get the pictures he needed and be back in his hotel within the hour.

Now all I need is a bit of little sister's luck.

Chapter Eight

J UAN LEANED BACK in his chair, listening as Micah Drake updated him on the information the team had received on Cooper Hicks. They'd known the man was a spook, but the full scope of his immersion in the murky world of the Central Intelligence Agency was slowly being pieced together. *Christ, the man isn't just ass deep in alligators, he's up to his neck and sinking fast.*

"Will they let him go?" Juan directed his question to Cameron Barnes, a *former* operative for the Agency, who was *anything but* former. Cam and his family had recently moved back to Texas and were currently putting the final touches on the major renovation of a large home nearby. It wasn't uncommon to find the man at Prairie Winds during the darkest hours before dawn—personally, Juan often wondered if the man was a vampire because it was much less common to see him during the daylight hours.

"Probably, but they'll do whatever they can to discourage it. He's too valuable." Running his hand through his hair in a clear sign of frustration, Cam shook his head and sighed. "Hell, he's barely taken a break from service since he signed on at eighteen. He has a photographic memory with an IQ that's one of the highest in the entire damned Agency. He'll be a walking target for years to come."

"That sounds like the voice of experience talking. Is this why they reel you in every now and again?" Juan saw the light of amusement in Cam's eyes at the implication.

"I started Dark Desires a few years before I officially retired, so I had another life established, and that made me somewhat more immune to the offers that came my way."

"*Somewhat?*" This time it was Kent who'd asked the question the rest of them were thinking.

"I'm not going to lie, the monetary propositions from not only Uncle Sam but many of the wealthiest nations in the world were staggering. I could have literally named my price, but there comes a time when money isn't enough. I had the club I'd established in Houston, and I threw myself headfirst into making it one of the best in the country. I also had a submissive I wasn't willing to leave for months at a time." The sly smile on the man's face said it all; it was common knowledge his love for Dr. Cecelia Barnes was his guiding force.

"The world was a different place when you walked away—a lot less volatile than it is now." Kyle's comment hadn't really been a question, but he was certainly trying to steer the conversation. Juan had known Kyle West for years, he didn't speak randomly, and he didn't speak unless he had a reason. Kyle's words always had a purpose.

"I know it appears that way on the surface, and I suppose it's true in the U. S., but this has been the norm in much of the world for many years. There is more at stake in our nation than the others because so much of the world's wealth is centered here."

"Other nations have decided it's long past time for them to share in our good fortune." Juan understood all the political backdoors as well as anyone, but he also knew most of it was created chaos, designed to benefit a few and cost the masses.

"They have been convinced it's their due, and the fires

of that anger have been fanned with religious rhetoric that isn't about faith at all. Don't think for a minute Cooper hasn't already been offered astronomical amounts of money for his help furthering the globalist agenda. These are not people who take no for an answer and let you walk away without using every resource available to them to change your mind." Cam was watching his words carefully, and that was almost as terrifying as where Juan's imagination was taking him. Deciding it was time to cut to the chase, Juan leveled a look at Cam.

"Do you think the attempt to pull Lakyn off the street was about gaining her brother's compliance?" If it was true, the game had been notched up a fucking hundred percent. Dealing with trained government operatives with unlimited funding was far different from some prick off the street with an overactive libido and lock picking set.

Cam leaned forward and shrugged. "I wish I knew for sure. That's part of the reason I'm here. I was hoping Cooper had made contact, I want to talk to him as soon as possible—maybe offer a word or two of advice." *A word or two of advice my ass*. Cam Barnes wasn't a fucking career counselor, if he was offering help, it was because he knew the man's life was on the line.

"I know he opened my last message but skipped all the previous ones." Kyle's words had barely been spoken when his phone chimed on the table in front of him. Picking it up, Kyle's expression turned grim. "Cooper needs an exit. He's been compromised." Turning his attention to Micah, he asked, "Who do we know that might be close enough to help?"

Cam, who was already tapping furiously on his phone, held up a finger. "Wait, I've got someone in London, and they're moving in to intercept now." What the hell? Juan had been in this meeting since Cam walked in and no one had ever given Cooper's exact location. Turning to Micah, Juan raised a brow in question. The other man shook his head and muttered several colorful curses before smiling ruefully.

"I've learned to not even ask. I'm not sure any of us want to know how he manages to track everybody on the damned planet. Fucking hell, I feel sorry for his children, and I want to call my parents and thank them for a stalking free childhood." Cam shot him a steely glare from across the room without his fingers ever slowing.

Juan shook his head as the room exploded into action around him. Wondering how this would play out for Lakyn, he couldn't help worrying about the woman sleeping peacefully back in their cabin, wrapped in Trac's arms—the lucky bastard. Within minutes, Cam's contact had not only intercepted Cooper Hicks but was already transporting the injured agent to a private medical facility on the outskirts of London. As Juan watched everything play out around him, he became more concerned than ever Lakyn was being used as bait—whether it was to draw Cooper out or force his compliance remained to be seen.

LAKYN WASN'T SURE what was going on, but Juan looked like he hadn't slept at all after their talk last night. She joined both men when they'd used what looked like a souped-up golf cart to go to the main house for breakfast. Walking into the dining room, she immediately sensed a strange tension filling the air. Kyle West was so deeply engrossed in his phone conversation, he didn't appear to notice his wife had moved from her seat beside him to sit down next to Lakyn.

"I hope you'll accept my apology for my behavior when you arrived. Good grief, I was so shocked, I was almost speechless. Dancing donuts, I wish I had been speechless. I'd never in a million years intentionally hurt someone I considered a friend." The sincerity in Tobi's eyes made Lakyn's eyes fill with unshed tears.

"Oh damn, please don't cry, it's contagious. You cry and I'll start, then the men will be all crazy trying to figure out what's happened, and I can tell you from unfortunate experience that never ends well for subs."

Lakyn couldn't hold back her giggle, *this* was the woman she'd been talking to. This version of Tobi West was familiar.

Tobi scanned the room, noting all the men huddled together talking or staring at various electronic devices.

"I don't know what's going on, but I'm all for taking advantage of it. The kids are going to spend the day with their grandfathers which means I'm free for the day. It's not supposed to get hot until later this afternoon, and I was thinking we could go tubing behind the house and gossip." The glint of mischief in Tobi's eyes made Lakyn wonder exactly what *tubing* entailed.

"Tubing?"

"We'll stay close because the guys will have a stroke if we venture beyond the property bordering Prairie Winds. We may own the adjoining down river property, but it isn't monitored as closely as the section behind the club. Of course, not monitored as closely is relative since even the wildlife has to request admittance... in triplicate... to anything Prairie Winds related." Tobi's eyes flashed with recognition when she looked over Lakyn's head and suddenly her hushed tone became much clearer.

"My husbands and the rest of the team take security very seriously, so we'll have to ask them about tubing, but I don't see why it would be a problem if we tether our tubes to the dock."

"You are incorrigible, sweetness. Tubing sounds like fun and since we're going to be tied up with work for several hours, you and Lakyn are welcome to play, under the following conditions." Lakyn suddenly became aware everyone in the room was watching the exchange. "You'll wear lifejackets." When Tobi opened her mouth, Kent shook his head. "No, darling wife, I don't give a flying fuck about tan lines. I do, however, lay awake at night, worrying about all the ways you might find to get into trouble, and given your love of all things water related, drowning is high on the list."

"Okay. Lifejackets. Drat."

Lakyn was betting this was an ongoing argument, and she wasn't inclined to get involved. At one time, she'd been an excellent swimmer, but she hadn't done anything more than lay on the beach and have her picture taken for years, so the added precaution was in her best interest.

"You'll also take a member of the team with you. Find somebody who isn't working today and ask them to accompany you." Tobi's eyes were shining and Lakyn wondered what she was up to. They'd only talked online, so she wasn't sure how to read Tobi's expressions. "We'll get a tracking bracelet for Lakyn before you go." His eyes softened when he looked pointedly at the diamond sparkler on his wife's wrist. Turning to Lakyn, Kent glanced over her shoulder to where Juan and Trac now stood.

"You'll check with your Doms before going to the river. Stay close, there hasn't been a lot of boat traffic yet this year, but that's bound to change. Remember, boats and tubes do not mix."

Lakyn felt like she'd fallen down a rabbit hole. Boats? Hadn't she heard Tobi mention boats? She didn't have any desire to battle a boat from a tube... good grief that would be crazy. Lakyn might be a lot of things, but suicidal wasn't one of them.

"We'll take Lakyn to Micah's office for the tracker, and one of us will accompany her to the dock." Trac helped her to her feet as he spoke, and when she reached for her plate, he gave her a knowing grin. She'd always seen Lakyn Storm as a completely different person apart from Lakyn Hicks. Her alter-ego might be a star, but even she knew better than to expect someone else to wait on her hand and foot. Picking up her dishes, she returned them to the kitchen and thanked the Wests' staff for a delicious breakfast.

Thirty minutes later, Lakyn wore a beautiful sapphire and diamond bracelet Micah Drake insisted was a *necessary precaution*. Personally, she thought they were nuts for allowing her to wear something so valuable in filthy river water, but it was obvious the point wasn't open for discussion. For a lovely piece of jewelry, it appeared to be remarkably functional. Not only would it send a continuous signal back to the Prairie Winds control center, giving her location, there was also a panic alarm. The small recessed button wouldn't be activated during normal use, but the wearer could press it, alerting the entire team if she needed help.

"As soon as this small button is locked down, the microphone begins transmitting a continuous audio stream which feeds to the entire team and is recorded at Prairie Winds. We'll hear everything happening around you." Micah flashed her a knowing smile. "While our contact back east was still perfecting it, a couple of the subs accidentally depressed the alarm while changing clothes in his club's locker room. Their conversation was recorded, and their Doms were not pleased with what they heard." His soft chuckle didn't do anything to soothe her sudden sense of unease.

"I don't think I want to wear this. It's too *Big Brother* for me. Thanks, but I think I'll pass." She wasn't about to have someone listening in on every conversation she had. Not having any personal privacy was one of the things she hated the most about her life in New York, but she'd at least had privacy in her own apartment... hadn't she? The next thing she heard was the sound of her own blood pounding in her ears and another man shouting about catching someone before she hit the ground.

What the hell was that about?

LUKE GRAYSON WALKED into the control center and was hit by a wave of emotion so strong, he had to reach out and grab the edge of a nearby desk to keep from stumbling. Lakyn Hicks was broadcasting panic so strongly, he wondered what the hell his boss had said to her. Juan Rivera and Trac Hughes skidded around the corner just as Micah was settling the petite beauty in a chair. Luke had been a member of the Prairie Winds team long enough to know the two men whose pale faces didn't look anything like the hardened warriors he knew they were. Their panic made it clear they considered her theirs. Pushing aside the emotions rolling off them, Luke took her hand and opened his mind to hers.

Luke's empathic gift was stronger than anyone else's in

his family, he also had better control over it—*usually*. Lakyn's mind was spinning so wildly out of control, it took him a few seconds to process the jumble of information flooding him. She'd been listening to Micah talk about the recording capabilities of the bracelet and suddenly realized she hadn't checked her apartment for hidden electronics after the break-ins.

"We'll take care of it, Lakyn. We'll have someone in there within the hour, I promise." Turning to Micah, Luke quickly explained her concern. His boss and mentor knelt in front of Lakyn and wrapped her free hand in his, her small hand swallowed up in Micah's giant mitts. Looking down where he held her hand in his, Luke realized for the first time how tiny she was. He laughed to himself, it was easy to forget how petite she was because she appeared bigger than life in all the photographs he'd seen.

Hell, this was the first time Luke had been this close to a woman whose beauty held the world captive, but touching her, he'd instantly known she was so much more than the person people saw when they looked at her picture in magazines or watched her on screen. When the men behind them growled, he cast a glare over his shoulder before turning back to give her a conspiratorial wink.

"There isn't any reason to worry about this now. We can't change the past, so let that go, but we might learn more about who broke into your apartment if they left some electronic goodies behind." Luke listened to her thoughts for a few more seconds, then satisfied she was on an even keel once again, he moved to his chair and rolled it smoothly to the bank of computers and got to work. He might be the youngest member of the team, but that didn't mean he was without resources, and one of those happened to live a few blocks from Lakyn's apartment building.

Luke met Brooklyn Adler when they were both students at MIT. As an only child, he'd been fascinated to learn his raven-haired lab partner was one of ten children, all named for places around the world. He and Brooklyn had become fast friends and they'd kept in touch after graduation. Luke always chuckled when he saw her business card in his wallet.

Brooklyn Adler

Insurance Acquisitions Specialist

He loved teasing her it was a fancy title for a licensed thief. B, as she was called by her friends and family, was a cat burglar extraordinaire. There wasn't a building she couldn't get into or a lock she couldn't open—and everyone he knew was more than a little grateful she used her skills for good rather than evil which she always swore would pay better.

Even though Luke had heard B talk about her large family, the only one of her siblings he'd met was her sister, Catalina. Brooklyn had explained her sister was a jewelry designer, but it hadn't taken Luke long to discover the real reason Cat was continually on the road.

Pushing those thoughts aside, Luke dialed B and smiled when it sounded as though she'd dropped the phone before answering. Brooklyn was a night owl and wasn't going to be thrilled about being awakened before noon, but it couldn't be helped.

"This better be life or fucking death, Luke… you *feel* what I'm saying, my friend?" Brooklyn knew about his gift and continually teased him, insisting he could make more money as a circus performer than as a computer specialist.

More than once, she'd pleaded with him to, at the very least, become a hacker, insisting he was going to die in the financial middle class—a fate she considered an unnecessary tragedy.

"Rise and shine, sweet cheeks, I need your help." He could feel her smile and hoped his bosses were prepared for what this was going to cost them. Brooklyn was the best, and she knew it—this wasn't going to be cheap. She wouldn't want money, but the favors she'd call in later would be huge.

Chapter Nine

"MY LIFE HAS turned into an unpublished tabloid story. People breaking into my apartment, stealing my underwear, and leaving who knows what DNA. Jerks trying to pull me into SUVs. Piece of shit rental cars. My brother and everybody else thinks I don't know what he does or who he works for, and now, some hot shot cat burglar is breaking into my apartment to find out what the last burglars left behind." Lakyn relaxed on the tube as much as anyone could, wrapped in a life preserver she was certain had been designed to save a drunken sailor drifting in hurricane tossed seas. Of course, the life vest inventor probably hadn't anticipated a group of Doms tying every safety device their former SEAL-selves could find to the obnoxious orange safety devices.

"I can help with the unpublished part. It would probably only take a phone call or two, but you're on your own with the rest of that nonsense. Now that I think about it, I think you should write a book. Hell, it probably wouldn't work, no one would believe it, and wouldn't that just piss you off?"

"What?"

"When they put it in the fiction section." Tobi's snark earned her a splash of river water, and Lakyn smiled to herself at the woman's high-pitched squeal. She was laughing so hard, she almost fell off the enormous tube that looked like it might swallow the tiny blonde whole. "You'll pay for that. If you fall off your tube, I'm going to let you drown, and with all the crap they've got tied on us, you're toast. I don't think these life jackets have a prayer of saving anyone." Truer words had never been spoken.

"Are you sure this rope is strong enough?" Lakyn was only half kidding. The rope looked awfully skimpy to her despite the reassurance of a man named Sam McCall whose wife was currently being fitted with her own arsenal.

"Jen said it's ski rope," Tobi shrugged, "but that doesn't mean anything to me. I asked for a jet ski for my birthday a couple of years ago, and I thought Kyle was going to have a stroke every time I mentioned it. When he heard his dads were going to buy one for me, he was apoplectic. Something about me attracting trouble." She shrugged innocently, but Lakyn wasn't falling for it, and Jen's hysterical laughter from the dock let them know she'd heard what Tobi had said.

"Seriously, Tobi? Even I would know better than to get you a jet ski. I heard about your last adventure on one, and as I recall, that ended with an explosion."

"Don't be a party-pooper. Stop playing grab-ass with Sam and get your fanny out here."

"Tobi, you are a menace, and you know perfectly well your Masters are going to hear your chatter." The man helping Jen into a tube was huge and intimidating as hell. Lakyn had been introduced to both Sam and Sage, but this was the McCall brother who scared her.

As if Tobi had read her mind, she looked at Lakyn and rolled her eyes.

"Do not and I repeat... do not show fear. They are like sharks... they can smell it like blood in the water, and they'll use it against you. Geez, Sam is a big softy, just like Kyle." She flashed the enormous man a smile as phony as any Lakyn had ever seen, then snickered when he growled at her.

Jen paddled her feet, trying to get closer to them, but the current had other ideas. "Good grief, I have so much tactical gear tied on me, I'm worried I might actually sink. And the one thing I asked for, they wouldn't give me."

"Pet, no one in their right mind was going to give you a trolling motor." Sam moved back to the shore and settled into a lounge chair Lakyn hadn't noticed under a nearby tree.

"Is he going to watch us the whole time?" Lakyn had tried to whisper, but she'd obviously misjudged how easily sound traveled over water.

"Yes, he is. He is going to sit right here and sip a fucking root beer because I need to keep my wits about me to deal with whatever trouble the three of you manage to attract."

"Three? What about me? My sons said my girl was down here tubing, and I want to play, too." Lakyn didn't know who the gorgeous middle-aged woman was, but if Tobi's squeal of happiness and Sam's groan were any indication, she was going to guess she was Lilly West. "Now be a dear and find me a tube, Sam. I'll wear a regular life jacket rather than one of those bulky ones, that's just overkill."

"Do your husbands know you are here, Mrs. West?"

Watching the sweet woman morph into a cross between the Wicked Witch of the West and Wonder Woman was fascinating. Lilly West could have made a fortune acting, but if Lakyn remembered correctly, Tobi said her mother-in-law had been a successful model before marrying two men.

"Sam, I *usually* like you. I'm somewhat surprised to hear you ask me that question." The look on Sam McCall's face told Lakyn he wasn't falling for Mrs. West's tap dance around the question.

"That won't work with me, Mrs. West. I'm not suiting you up without talking to one of your men."

"You're a brave man, Sam." A very distinguished look-ing man ambled around a hedge into view, and Lilly's entire face lit up when he looked her way. "My love, are you stirring up trouble? You know how Del gets when you're being ornery, and since he is currently being out-maneuvered by our lovely granddaughter, he'll be particu-larly difficult to deal with this evening." Lakyn was mesmerized by the man's interaction with his wife. It was easy to see where Kent West got his charm… holy cats.

After a brief discussion, Sam dropped the lifejacket over Lilly's head and began securing the numerous straps and buckles. Tobi and Jen moved closer to the dock, chattering a mile a minute with Lilly while Lakyn drifted further out in the river as she studied the rock cliff on the opposite side.

The geological formations drew her attention, and she paddled closer, taking up a lot of the slack in the rope tethering her to the dock. Lakyn had done a photo shoot at the Grand Canyon a couple of years earlier, and she'd felt drawn to the layers marking of the passage of time in eons rather than days or weeks. The wall she was facing now had some of the same layering and before she realized how far she'd drifted, she was almost in the middle of the river and so lost in thought, she didn't hear the approaching boat until it was close… really close.

Everything slowed down, just like it did in the movies,

and Lakyn scanned the area around her, looking for a way to avoid being hit by the oncoming speedboat. Glancing toward the dock, she saw Sam waving frantically at her, and she could hear the echoes of Tobi and Jen screaming for her to come back. When she looked at the approaching boat, she knew it was too late, she'd never reach the dock in time. For a few seconds, she thought the looming craft was going to skirt around her, but one look at the man behind the wheel, and she knew he intended her harm.

The leer on the driver's face was frightening, and she held her breath waiting for the blow she knew was coming. The man behind the wheel wore dark clothing, and there was something familiar about him, but she didn't have time to think about it as she watched him veer sharply to his right cutting between her and the dock. For a split second, Lakyn thought she'd be okay, but the reprieve was short-lived as the boat's propeller tangled with the rope holding her to the dock. She felt the moment the thin nylon rope snapped, and the tube was almost yanked out from under her as it was pulled behind the speeding boat.

Lakyn frantically began trying to free herself from the tube, but the force of the boat pulling her faster and faster along the water and all the crap they'd tied to her life preserver made it difficult to maneuver. The driver started weaving back and forth, causing the rope to sail her in an ever-widening arc, reminding her of her friends playing crack the whip when they'd all gone ice skating. She suspected he was planning to swing her into the rock cliff without driving his boat near the shallow rocks.

Sam McCall had warned her not to venture past the boundary of the Prairie Winds property under any circumstances and described the marker she'd already sailed past. Everyone had made such a production of pointing out the facility's boundaries, Lakyn assumed her tracking bracelet only worked if she was within those confines.

God only knew how long it would take them to find her now that she'd been pulled much farther downstream. Finally remembering the small tool Sam had tucked in the pocket of her life preserver, she pulled it free and sliced the rope just before she hit the peak of the arc nearest the shore. The force sent her tube skipping over the water like a stone, but Lakyn's relief at being free from the boat was short-lived when she realized she didn't have any way to stop. Why the hell did Tobi's husband think tubes were safer? Jet skis were far easier to control. *Damn!*

Years of training kicked in, and Lakyn tucked her chin against her chest and crossed her arms over her face, protecting what her team always told her was her most valuable asset. The emptiness of that realization slammed into her chest a split second before the tube lodged in thick reeds along the river, sending her sailing through the air.

SAM CAUGHT HIS wife as she tried to sprint past him. When she'd seen the boat bearing down on Lakyn, Jen had shed her life jacket like the trained operator she was and bailed off her tube. She'd been close enough to the shore, she'd literally hit the ground running heading to the small shed here the Wests stored the team's small helicopter.

"Where do you think you're going?" Sam growled the question but didn't expect her to answer—hell, they both knew exactly what she planned to do, and the last thing he needed was Jen going off half-cocked without back-up.

His earpiece crackled to life and his brother chuckled, "Let her go, I'm already doing the pre-flight checks. Can't say I've ever had a co-pilot wearing a polka-dot bikini before, but I'm not going to complain."

Christ, just what he needed, his horny brother and their wild-child wife locked together in a glass bubble a thousand feet above the ground.

Threading his hands through her wet hair, Sam crushed his lips against hers in a heated kiss before pulling back. "Be careful." He gave mostly bare ass a swat, the wet skin giving a satisfying pop against his palm, before he watched her run the short distance to where Sage waited. Sending up a silent prayer of thanks to whoever invented thong swimsuits, Sam turned to see Tobi trying to sneak by him on her way to the jet skis tied at the far side of the dock.

"Freeze, Tobi." Jesus, Joseph, and Mary, what was with the subs today? Was it some sort of special full moon or something? *Damn.*

A cart holding several team members skidded to a stop at the end of the dock. Juan and Trac ran for the jet skis as they pulled the tabs on their self-inflating tactical vests. By the time they'd untied the jet skis, Sage and Jen were lifting off. The roar of the watercraft engines sounded over the whoop-whoop of the helicopter's rotor, and Sam looked over to see both Del and Dean West sheltering Lilly from the noise. In a flash of insight, Sam saw his future. Jen would always want to be right in the thick of things, and no matter how old he and Sage were, they'd always protect her. Just as Lilly stood between Dean and Del, they'd keep Jen between them because that was exactly where she belonged. *Christ, didn't Dean say Del was with Kodi?* Both Kodi and Kameron West were brilliant children, but Kodi was hell on wheels, just like her mother. Sam hoped like hell she hadn't followed her grandfather to the river—*I need a fucking raise.*

Tobi stood on the river bank, glaring his way with her arms crossed over her chest, emphasizing the cleavage so prominently displayed.

"Hell, one deep breath and she's going to come out of that top." Kent's amused voice sounded from beside him, and Sam had to agree. "If we weren't in the middle of a— well, never mind. Let's get Lakyn back, then I'm going to torture my sub until she admits why her breasts have grown, and she was drinking virgin margaritas the other night."

Sam couldn't hold back his laughter because it was a running joke that only at Prairie Winds was pregnancy contagious.

CAMERON BARNES LOOKED down at the luscious bare ass peaked perfectly over his lap and smiled. His sub was vibrating with need, and she still had several swats to go. The sass she'd given him before the last of the construction crew left had earned her a spanking he was more than happy to provide. Just as he raised his hand to finish the last series of swats, his phone's emergency alarm sounded. *Fucking hell.*

"Up you go, Pet." He handed her off to her other Master and pulled his phone out, answering it with one word, "Barnes." Micah Drake's clipped words sent Cam running out the back door as he shouted instructions over his shoulder to Carl. Hell, they hadn't even finished moving in, and their neighbors were already causing trouble.

Laughing to himself, Cam easily found the woman half of the Prairie Winds team was currently searching for.

Lakyn Hick's entire body was covered in mud, grass, and sand. If the scowl on her pretty face was any indication, Cam bet she had sand in a few places it didn't belong as well.

"Hello, beautiful. Nice of you to drop by." He smiled down at her and chuckled when she blinked up at him in confusion. "Wondering how I got here before anyone else, Lakyn?"

"Not really. I learned a long time ago CIA agents have some sort of built-in trouble detector... well, Cooper's *usually* works... not so much lately." Cam was shocked by her admission since they'd all doubted she knew who her brother worked for. When he didn't respond right away, she didn't bother to elaborate and simply held up her hand in a silent request for help to her feet.

Shaking his head, he knelt beside her. "No, you stay right where you are until the Calvary arrives." She started brushing the debris from her arms and legs, wincing when she encountered a sharp piece of reed stuck in her thigh. "I'm going to play the security footage back to see how you managed to keep your face perfectly clean and uninjured when the rest of you looks like you rode a tube through a jungle before being rolled in mud and sand."

"Years of training." For just a second, Cam caught a glimpse of the vulnerable woman beneath the star persona and hoped Juan and Trac were up to the task of convincing Lakyn the world would benefit from her intelligence even more than it had from her pretty face.

"How long have you known about Cooper?" He could hear the whirl of the helicopter and the high-pitched whine of the jet skis as they closed in.

"You mean how long have I known he wasn't a SEAL anymore? Or how long have I known he'd been recruited by the Agency?" Sighing, she shook her head. "I swear to all things holy, I hope to hell I don't look as dim as everyone assumes I am. It's just plain insulting." Cam leaned his head back and laughed.

"Beautiful, you are going to fit right in at Prairie Winds." Hovering over her, Cam blocked the flying sand as Sage set the chopper down. He'd read her file and knew she was as smart as she was gorgeous, but files rarely give you a sense of a subject's personality, and Cam was happy to see she would fit in so well with the other submissives. His own sub was going to be taking a lot more time off in the near future, so she'd have ample opportunity to spend time with the other submissives at Prairie Winds. He knew she'd missed having friends while they'd lived in St. Maarten, and that had played a large part in his and Carl's decision to move their family back to Texas.

"What is it with Texas and blowing sand?" He'd barely heard her question as pandemonium broke out around them. Juan and Trac were at her side within seconds, and Cam happily turned her over to them. He'd heard the story of how the men had found her on the edge of the road and chuckled to himself at her frustration with the wind and blowing dirt in Texas. *Just wait until the first time she gets run over by a tumbleweed stampede.*

Chapter Ten

COOPER LIMPED OUT of the small hospital, barely quelling the string of profanity threatening to color the air around him. The woman who'd pulled him from the alley hours ago sat idly behind the wheel of the car, a brow raised in silent challenge. How the hell had Cam Barnes managed to send the one woman in the entire world Cooper had hoped like hell he'd never have to see again? Catalina Adler was the bane of his existence, and this was the second time in the past six months she'd been sent to save his bacon.

"You don't look much better, Ace. Maybe you should limp back in there and give it another go." The husky tone of her voice only added fuel to the fire of her criticism and made him wish he could tie her to a St. Andrew's cross and flog her until the sass she wore like armor evaporated into a heated mist.

"Thanks for your concern, Princess, but I think I've been properly medicated to deal with your driving." She appreciated being called Princess almost as much as he liked being called Ace, so they could call this particular point a draw. Shaking her head, Cat started the car and drove sedately away from the small clinic. When he leveled a curious look at her, she gave him an unimpressed shrugged.

"There's no reason to draw unnecessary attention by

tearing out of here like our asses are on fire. Cam was crystal clear in his expectations. I'm supposed to make sure the docs patch you up, then deliver you to the airfield. You'll be stateside before your handler knows you've disappeared."

Cat was anything but naïve, and she knew as well as he did, his handler had likely given the order for his takedown in the alley. He'd been hurt, but not seriously enough for it to be seen as anything more than a warning. Ironically, it only reinforced his resolve to walk away. It gave him a great deal of satisfaction to know he'd inflicted more damage on the three men who'd jumped him than he'd suffered at their hands. Settling down in his seat and pulling the bill of his hat down to keep the rays of the rising sun from blinding him, Cooper didn't respond. *Why bother? She's right and agreeing with her would be tantamount to throwing gas on a fire.*

"There's no need to sulk, you know. I was nearby, and God knows I owe Cam more than a few favors though I have to admit, I find it interesting the Prairie Winds team calls in two favors from my family in one night."

Don't take the bait. Do. Not. Take. The. Bait.

"I pulled ambulance duty, and B got a call from one of her college pals to break into some celebrity's apartment near her place to look for bugs." The hair on the back of Cooper's neck stood straight up in warning. He knew where Brooklyn Adler lived, and it was damned close to Lakyn's small apartment.

Catalina sighed heavily as she glanced at him slumped beside her. Her knowing look made his jaw clench so tight, he might well shatter a tooth or two. Only a handful of people at the Agency knew about his sister, and Cat Adler wasn't on the short list—or at least she shouldn't be. When he didn't respond, she shook her head in frustration.

"You don't have to like me to trust me, Cooper. I have four sisters and five brothers. Hell, I'm the last person who would ever sell out someone's sibling." For the first time since he'd gotten in the car, Cooper turned his full attention to Catalina and wondered what the woman behind the snark was really like. She was an enigma—that was a given. He knew she worked for the Agency, but he'd gotten the distinct impression her work was more free-lance than as a career agent.

Globetrotting as one of the most sought-after jewelry designers in the world was a perfect cover, letting her breeze in and out of countries while no one looked at her twice. Okay, that was a lie, but those of us looking aren't thinking about espionage. Studying her profile, Cooper wondered what her real hair color was since it was different every time he saw her. *Makes me wonder what else is a mirage?*

Taking a deep breath and wincing at the pain shooting through his broken ribs, Cooper decided to take a chance. "Did Brooklyn find any bugs in Lakyn's apartment?"

This time the look she gave him was tinged with sympathy and understanding. "Yeah, she did. The place was loaded. She left to call it in, and they sent her back to tap in, so the Prairie Winds control center can try to follow the signals back to their source, but she said the stuff is really sophisticated, so it's not going to be a cakewalk."

"Fucking hell." If Brooklyn Adler thought the devices were advanced, they were cutting edge. "I finally got to check my messages while I waited for the doctor to show up, and Lakyn said she was having trouble with a stalker."

"A stalker with access to technology only a few agencies in the world can get their hands on? Seems unlikely, don't you think?" Yeah, he thought it was a fucking stretch, too, but once again, he was reluctant to agree with Cat, just on principle. "How did Prairie Winds get involved in this? Seems a bit outside of their usual repertoire." That was a million-dollar question and one he was more than a little interested in himself.

"I'm looking forward to hearing the answer to that myself. But you know how it is with siblings, just when you think you have them figured out, they come at you from left field."

Catalina snorted, and he barely heard her muttered, "Preach" before she took the turn into the small airfield on two wheels. Fucking hell, the woman missed her calling, she should have been a Formula One driver.

Of all the places in the country, how had his conscientious sister managed to find herself under the protection of one of the best teams of operatives in the world? Hell, he didn't even want to think about how she was coping with the Wests' kink club. Ordinarily, Lakyn was so predictable, she was almost boring—or at least as boring as a celebrity could be. If it wasn't work-related, she didn't do it. His sister had a work ethic that rivaled his own. Hell, now that he thought about it, they were both boring.

LAKYN ROLLED HER eyes when Juan asked her for the fifth time if she was steady enough to walk on her own the short distance to the SUV they'd be taking back to Prairie Winds. She'd politely assured him... *again*... she was capable of walking a few feet, but Trac hadn't missed her gesture of frustration. His eyes narrowed, and his glare might have been intimidating any other day, but after the scare she'd just had, his glower was easy to ignore. At least his narrowed eyes and frown hadn't meant much until he reached behind her and gave her ass a solid smack with his open palm.

"Hey, what the hell was that for?"

"Don't roll your eyes at your Dom even if you are annoyed he's asking you the same question over and over." She started to roll her eyes at his terse remark but quickly schooled her expression. "Good save, Princess. Now let's get you home and cleaned up before the briefing."

"Briefing?" She honestly couldn't imagine what anyone thought she could contribute when she'd been scared out of her mind. *Not exactly conducive to information gathering.* The ride back to the cabin seemed remarkably short compared to the terrifying trip she'd made going the other direction. Lakyn could only imagine how intense the briefing would be… if the interrogations she'd endured with her brother were any indication, it was going to be a long afternoon.

JUAN KNEW LAKYN was crashing, it was written all over her. He and Trac flanked her in the back seat while one of the new recruits drove them back to the small cabin they called home. Trac looked at him over her head and raised a brow. Yeah, they were definitely on the same page, she was fading fast. Leaning against him, Lakyn's eyes slowly slid closed, and he looked down to see her shivering. Carl and CeCe had wrapped her in a blanket before they left the Barnes' new home, but these shivers didn't have anything to do with being chilled. When they parked in front of the cabin, Trac held her upright while Juan stepped out and quickly turned to slide arms under Lakyn's petite form. She was feather-light in his arms, making it easy for him to cradle her in his embrace.

Relieved she hadn't protested being carried, Juan moved through the cabin without stopping until he could gingerly sit her on the counter. Trac started the water in the large jetted tub, and they both stripped in record time. Juan carefully unwrapped her from the blanket and loosened the ties of her bikini.

"It's like unwrapping the most beautiful gift I've ever received."

"Hell, even battered and bruised, she's fucking gorgeous. I'm glad Del and Dean's security is linked to the club's, I'm looking forward to finding out who did this to you, Princess." Trac's voice sounded as strained as Juan felt. The elder Wests lived on a parcel of land bordering Prairie Winds which was convenient for many reasons.

When the first radio call came in that Lakyn was being towed on a fucking tube down the river by an unknown, Juan and Trac had both panicked. Thank God the building where they'd been training was close to the back of the Wests' property, bordering the river. He and Trac had been on jet skis heading downstream in less than two minutes.

Pushing aside thoughts of anything but the woman in the oversized tub between his legs with her back pressed against his chest, Juan watched Trac use his hands to spread shower gel over her arms and legs. The lifejacket she'd been wearing might have felt like overkill to Lakyn, but it had offered her chest and back some measure of protection.

Trac lovingly squirted the floral smelling gel into his hands and rubbed them together until they were covered with bubbles before smoothing the frothy suds over her breasts. Rolling her peaked nipples between his slick fingers, Trac grinned when she groaned and arched into his touch.

"Not yet, Princess. We're going to use this as a lesson. You need to be more careful—your safety is and always will be our priority. Sam said you'd drifted away from the others, and that's how the driver of the boat was able to skim over the rope." The outboard motor had easily snapped the rope and wrapped it tight enough to pull her the mile she'd traveled downstream.

"I think you are looking at this all wrong. If we'd all been grouped together, he probably would have run over one of my new friends to get to me. I think I deserve a reward for looking out for the safety of the group. There's probably some sort of civic recognition in my future. Heck, I'll bet the Governor shows up to present me with a plaque, after all, I saved two citizens from disaster." Juan had to bite his tongue to keep from laughing out loud. Lakyn was quick-witted even through the fog of a steep fall into an adrenaline crash.

By the time they all got dressed and drove back to the main house, Kent and Kyle's office was overflowing with people. Micah waved them up closer to Kyle's desk and motioned for them to take the two chairs closest to a large monitor. When Lakyn looked confused, Juan smiled and pulled her down onto his lap.

"Subs often sit on cushions at their Master's feet at the club, but you'll find Trac and I prefer having you on our lap."

Micah leaned close and grinned, "And I want you to be able to see the spliced footage between the three security systems, sweetness. You did us proud." By this time, Kent

West had joined them, and his eyes were practically dancing with mirth.

"Damn, Lakyn, do you perform your own stunts? Because I have to tell you, I was damned impressed. What are you doing traveling all over the world letting those fashion yo-yos take your picture when we could use you on the teams?"

"Oh, fuck no." Juan felt his usual charm evaporate in a heated mist. "She is not joining the teams. No. Just. Fucking. No." For the first time since this whole disaster started two hours ago, he heard laughter all around him and realized how close to the edge of imploding he sounded.

LAKYN WATCHED THE video play on the enormous monitor and felt the strangest sense of detachment until she looked at the stricken look on Juan and Trac's faces. Sam McCall had stepped to the side of the large screen to point out various points, and when he finished, she was surprised when the entire process started again, this time with Cameron Barnes adding his analysis. Jen McCall took the third round and when she'd finished, Kyle turned to her.

"Lakyn, we're going to run it through again at half-time, and I'd like you to walk us through it from your point of view." She must have looked confused because his expression softened, and he added, "We want to know what you were thinking before you realized the boat was bearing down on you and every moment thereafter. Consider it a "thought map." We'll probably hear things you don't even realize you're saying—I know it sounds strange, but you're going to have to trust me just this once."

This once? Was he delusional? She instinctively trusted every former soldier in the room because they all reminded her of Cooper. Just thinking about her older brother made her eyes fill with tears, but she blinked them back, refusing to give in to emotion. The team needed her perspective and from the way they were acting, the whole situation was more serious than she'd first believed.

Damn it, Cooper, where the hell are you?

Chapter Eleven

L AKYN WATCHED THE video and tried to remember what she'd been thinking at various points, but it was difficult to remember when all she could think about was how scared she'd been. Hell, she'd been sure the jack ass driving the boat was going to find his window of opportunity to fling her into the rocks before she could pull her fat ass out of the tube. She hadn't realized she'd spoken aloud until Trac leaned over and whispered, "That's ten, Princess."

They took the rule about subs not making disparaging comments about themselves to a ridiculous level if you asked her, but she wasn't going to add bricks to her sinking ship by telling them so. As soon as the video switched to Cameron Barnes cameras, he stepped forward and began asking questions rather than waiting for her to walk them through it.

"It looks like the driver yells something to you, Lakyn. I want you to close your eyes and put yourself back on that tube for a moment. Let's rewind a few seconds, shall we?" She thought he was talking about the video, so she opened her eyes. "No, sweet girl, you keep those eyes closed."

Lakyn was speechless. Not only did she keep her eyes open, but she was standing toe to toe with Cameron Barnes before Juan had been able to stop her.

"We met at the hospital. The night I had my appendix

out. You were there... but you were older. How is that possible?" A snort of laughter from the back of the room caught Lakyn's attention, and she looked up to see Mia waving her arm in the air like an errant school kid.

"Ask me... ask me. I know this one."

Tucker Deitz looked at his wayward sub and rolled his eyes. "Kodak, you're going to find yourself over my lap in about a half a heartbeat if you don't pipe down." Mia didn't seem terribly intimidated, and when she mouthed the word *later* to Lakyn, it had been hard to hold back her laughter.

"What Mia is trying—inappropriately, perhaps—to tell you is I'm ordinarily quite good with disguises although I'll admit I don't seem to have done a stellar job with the two of you since you've both remembered one of my favorite alter egos." Lakyn almost laughed at the frown lines forming between his brows as he seemed to be considering the implications of that.

"You told me you were a friend of Cooper's and you stayed with me until he got home. The doctors listened to you." Laughter erupted around her.

"Yes, well, I can be very persuasive, sweet girl. I mentored your brother, so looking out for you until he could get back to New York was important to him, and you needed an advocate because God knows that worthless manager of yours wasn't doing anything." Lakyn was so shocked by his words, she felt herself sway before Juan pulled her back down onto his lap.

"Princess, we keep hearing the same thing over and over about your manager, perhaps it's time to cut him loose." Cameron Barnes looked at Trac and shook his head.

"Love turns men to mush. This is the reason Special

Forces commanders don't want their man to fall in love." His words might have sounded harsh, but the tenderness reflected in his eyes let her know there was a kind heart hiding beneath the harsh exterior. As if he'd read her mind, he shook his head, "Let's get back to my question. Do you remember what the man shouted, Lakyn?"

Closing her eyes, she tried to visualize the scene in her mind, letting the sounds and smells flood her senses. Her mind had blocked some details, but watching it play out on the monitor had helped pull those bits and pieces back to the forefront.

"The motor was so loud, I could barely hear him, but I know he said something about brother and council." Frowning she strained to pull it all back, but there was something just out of her reach. "Could you run it back, frame by frame?"

"Absolutely." They restarted the video, and she leaned so far forward, she almost scooted herself off Juan's knees.

"When is the last time you had your eyes checked, *Cariña*?" Waving him off, she wasn't about to tell him how badly she needed the contacts they hadn't given her time to put in before leaving the cabin. *Yeah, you wouldn't want to ride in a car with me driving right now, that's for sure.* A snort of laughter from her side made Lakyn turn in that direction. When the man stepped close enough for her to see him, she wanted to sink into the floor.

"How long have you been here?" She hadn't intended for the question to sound so harsh, but she hated the thought he'd been listening in on her unmonitored thoughts.

"I've been standing here the entire time—something you would know if you were wearing your contacts. It's not safe for you to go without them, you know, and I noted you didn't have on a hat or sunglasses when you were tubing."

What the hell? Does this guy work for the Wests or the Surgeon General? When he laughed, she felt her face flush.

"I work for the Wests although I'm sure the Surgeon General would agree that you should be wearing eye protection and sunscreen."

I swear on my mother's grave I'd slap him silly, but he'd know it was coming.

Trac cleared his throat, and when Lakyn looked at him, she was surprised to see him glaring at her. "I'm tired of hearing half of this conversation." Pointing at Luke, he frowned, "Being a part of the team means you share the information."

"What he really means is the Doms stick together and rat out the subs at every opportunity." Lakyn didn't even need to turn around to recognize Jen McCall's voice.

"Rat out? Really, Jennifer?" Cam gave her a reproving look. "For a former diplomat, your vocabulary is seriously lacking."

"Damn, you're right. Snitch? Tattle? Narc? Help me out here, I'm out of my element."

"You're going to be out of your element if you don't knock it off." This time Lakyn did turn to the trio sitting directly behind her, just in time to see Sam McCall give his pretty wife a glacial look. Jen's other husband was shaking his head as if he'd given up trying to keep her out of trouble.

"Lakyn," Kyle West stepped forward and nodded to the monitor, "if you'll try to ignore the troublemakers in the peanut gallery and re-focus your attention on the screen. I'd suggest you wear your contacts or glasses in the future as a safety precaution. Not only do you need to be able to protect yourself from abduction, it will probably help you avoid a paddling or two." She resisted the urge to roll her eyes at the laughter she heard all around her. Kyle shook his head and glared over her head. "Don't let them bait you, Lakyn."

"That's it." She felt her eyes widen as the piece of the puzzle she'd been trying to grasp popped into her head. "He said something about a council and called me bait. That was the word I heard just as I cut the rope."

JUAN ESCORTED LAKYN into the kitchen where several of the other submissives were gathered around an elaborate spread that looked like they planned to feed an army.

"I don't know who is responsible for the buffet, but I hope you take time to enjoy it while I drive down to the cabin and get your contacts." He gave her a reprimanding look he hoped kept her from arguing. Juan might not be the strictest Dom at the club, but he wouldn't let a challenge go unmet, especially one issued in front of other club members.

"Thank you. Everything I'll need is in my purse." A flash of unease reflected in her amazing eyes, but she shuttered it quickly, reminding him why her acting skills had made her a world-recognized celebrity.

"When is the last time you checked in with your manager, *Cariña*?" Even though he wasn't anxious for her to return to work, he doubted she would be happy sitting back on her laurels for long.

"The day before I left. It seems odd he hasn't been blowing up my phone. I know he isn't a great manager, but he usually checks in regularly to update me on offers he's screening or contracts he's forwarding to my attorney. He also updates my calendar online, but ordinarily, calls to confirm I've seen his additions and changes." When he cocked a brow at her in questions, she shrugged. "I had planned to take a month off, but after that short hiatus, I'm stacked for the next two years. After that I want to see where things lead."

"Stacked?" Juan agreed that she was stacked, but he doubted her meaning was the same as his.

"Seven days a week. I won't have more than a half day off for a little over two years." He heard several of the women around them gasp, and he was equally surprised.

"Damn, girl, have you signed all those contracts already? Because I have to tell you, that's just not healthy." Tobi leaned on the counter beside Juan, and he appreciated the little fireball calling her friend out.

"Most of them are just verbal commitments at this point, so I may be able to pare it down some so I can work on my fashion line."

"I thought the new fashion line was your passion? Why are you putting off your dream? Life's too short to spend it doing something your heart isn't in." Damn, Juan needed to remember to send Tobi a huge bouquet of her favorite flowers for all her help. "I'll bet you have a kazillion dollars stashed *just in case*, don't you? You're one of those people who plans themselves into a deep rut because something disrupted their life as a kid." Tobi's words brought a sheen of tears to Lakyn's eyes, but she didn't deny the assessment. Juan's sisters had trained him well, and he recognized a good exit point when he saw one.

"I'll be right back, *Cariña*. Listen to what your friends have to say, it's always good to get the perspective of people who don't stand to gain financially from your decisions. I'll be back in a few minutes." Pressing a quick kiss to her lips, Juan sent Trac a quick text, letting him know he was heading back to the cabin. The terse note he received in return told him how close his friend was teetering to the edge of his control.

TRAC WAS CONVINCED his blood pressure was going to cause him to have a stroke any minute. Not only had someone tried to pull Lakyn off the street in New York, there had been another attempt today—this one intent on sending her brother a message, and it happened right under their noses. As a SEAL, Trac had always understood, at the end of the day, his job was to protect those who couldn't protect themselves, and he couldn't remember a time he felt like more of a failure.

The biggest draw for him as a sexual Dominant wasn't the sex, it was the intense connection between him and the submissive who gifted him with her trust. His desire to protect Lakyn was exponentially greater than anything he'd ever felt before, and seeing that damned video play over and over, highlighting how close they'd come to losing her had been a test he wasn't prepared for.

The driver had been a pro—he'd known exactly what he was doing, and his calculations for the timing and arc it would take to throw Lakyn into the jagged rockface wall had been dead on. The only mistake he'd made was underestimating the woman. Thank God Sam McCall had insisted each of the women had a way to cut herself free should her lifejacket become entangled in hooks on the tube or in the brush both above and below the surface of the fast-moving water.

Kyle West leaned back in his enormous leather office chair and frowned. "It pisses me off we allowed these fuckers to bring this bullshit to our door." Every man in the room froze. While Kyle wasn't above cursing, it was unusual to hear him lace a single sentence with so much colorful language. Even his brother seemed surprised. Rolling his eyes, Kyle chuckled, "Christ, have I become such a pansy-ass you're all speechless when I cuss?"

"Yeah, pretty much, extra emphasis on the pansy part." Kent's grin was contagious, and Trac felt the tension in his muscles begin to ebb away. Leaning close to him, Kent grasped his shoulder. "We'll keep her safe, brother. They overplayed their hand, and we've already got a lead on the driver." Trac looked over at his friend and boss, waiting for more information, but Kent nodded toward Kyle.

"Our groundwork is paying off in spades, we've got a solid lead on the prick behind the wheel. It seems he's a merc and isn't choosy about who he works for. The guy at the boat rental company is a friend of ours, and he was more than happy to provide us with their security footage. Between Micah and Phoenix, we had a name within minutes. James Cox is his real name, but his list of aliases is as long as your damned arm." Trac knew Phoenix Morgan and Micah Drake had developed a kick-ass facial recognition program and was thrilled they were using it to help identify Lakyn's assailant. Maybe with a little luck, they could place the guy in New York as well.

"The alias list is a prereq for a mercenary." Kent's nonchalant shrug earned him a glare from Kyle.

"I'm waiting to talk to Cooper—hopefully, he'll have some idea who is targeting Lakyn. Cam arranged Coop's travel home, and he's due to arrive late tonight. We're hoping to get him onsite before his handler knows he is no longer in London." What Kyle *wasn't* saying was almost as clear as what he'd said.

Jen McCall pushed away from the window where she'd been standing and asked, "Am I the only one who thinks we might be dealing with two factions?" She seemed torn about whether she should continue, but a quick nod from Sam was all the encouragement she'd needed. "We've all worked for Uncle Sam, and I think we'll all agree the government often does things we don't necessarily agree with. But intentionally kidnapping a U.S. citizen or slinging a woman into a rock wall seems like a stretch even for the C.I.A." Trac agreed, but the look on Cam's face wasn't encouraging. *Fucking hell.*

Chapter Twelve

LAKYN LISTENED AS Tobi, Gracie, and Mia all encouraged her to rethink her two-year plan. Their arguments were solid, but it was going to take a while for her heart to catch up with their logic. Tobi set her tablet on the counter between them and quickly brought up the sketches Lakyn had sent during their conversations.

"Look at these, Gracie. Our friend is damned talented, and I'd love to see what she could come up with for club wear because these are already edgy."

The women fussed over the designs, and Lakyn felt herself being drawn into their enthusiasm for the breadth of possibilities if she expanded her portfolio. Knowing Tobi and Gracie would help her get the exposure she'd need in the specialty market of fet-wear was a huge plus. Gracie grabbed Lakyn's forearm and gave it a reassuring squeeze. The pretty Latino woman took a sip of her wine and turned to Lakyn, a question dancing in her eyes.

"What will your brother say if you start designing dresses with cutouts that allow a woman's nipples to show? Is he a prude? Prudes don't usually appreciate much about the lifestyle." The pretty woman's eyes were beginning to glaze over, and Lakyn laughed when Gracie's loud hiccup seemed to surprise her.

"Great, my business partner is toasted. Real nice, Gracie. Way to be compassionate to those of us who can't," Tobi's eyes darted around the room, and she quickly amended, "I mean, those of us who don't actually like wine." Winking at Lakyn, she turned her attention to the bottle of water in her hand and frowned.

"I'm glad Cooper wasn't badly hurt. Have you heard from him, Lakyn?" Mia's words were slightly slurred, and Lakyn might have found it amusing if she hadn't been so shocked by what her friend had said. When she didn't respond, Mia looked at Tobi and flinched. "Shit. I'm really no good at all this spy stuff. I need to stick with pictures. Despite that damned saying about pictures being worth a thousand words, they really don't talk. Pickle fudge, I'm going to be in so much trouble."

Lakyn didn't say a word and didn't want to put her friends in the unenviable position of being forced to lie to her, so she simply turned on her heel and headed back to the Wests' office. It wasn't far, but her transformation from recovering victim and target to pissed off celebrity had taken place between one heartbeat and the next. Knocking once, she didn't wait for an invitation before walking into the room with her head held high, shoulders back, and steam rolling out her ears.

All eyes turned to her as she marched through the room, but the only person who said anything was Luke Grayson. His quickly whispered, "Oh shit" was the only thing she heard until she let Trac see how betrayed she felt, then turned her frosty glare on Kyle West.

"Where is my brother, and what's happened to him?" Kyle stood and started to move around his desk, but she put up her hand, stilling his movement. "Let me be crystal clear here, Mr. West, you are no longer dealing with the shaken woman who slid ashore on Mr. Barnes property. You're dealing with a very pissed off sister who has the patience of a provoked rattlesnake when she's being yanked around. I deal with people trying to blow smoke up my ass all the time, so don't even try to placate me." When Trac stood and moved closer, she used the same hand to halt his advance as well.

"Don't. Just don't." She was so angry, she was practically vibrating with it and could feel tears beginning to pool in her eyes. She cursed under her breath at the wave of emotion building so fast, it was threatening to break her into a thousand pieces.

The room was deathly quiet, and no one appeared to be prepared to answer her question until Jen McCall looked around the room and shook her head.

"I tried to tell you this was going to happen. You can't play it like this with intelligent women. Damn." Shifting her attention to Lakyn, Jen met her gaze without flinching. "Your brother is fine, Lakyn. He got worked over, night before last, but he was checked out before hopping a plane and heading here. He'll be here later tonight."

Lakyn fell back into a chair, feeling like a puppet whose strings had been cut. The flood of relief knowing Cooper was all right had been more than her trembling knees could stand. It took her a few seconds to pull in enough oxygen to push back the black dots dancing in her vision. She stood again before anyone could move to her side and once again, faced the men she felt had misled her.

"Tobi told me several times how important honesty was at the Prairie Winds Club... how critical communication... honest communication was to a successful D/s relationship." She took a couple steadying breaths before continuing. When she looked up, Juan was standing in the doorway. The stricken look on his face almost stole her resolve, but she turned her attention back to the Wests and

Cameron Barnes.

"Respect is a two-way street, gentlemen, and trust is earned. Don't ask for something you aren't willing to give. I have to wonder if you really are friends with Cooper because I've never known him to spend time with anyone whose integrity I believed could be called into question." She saw them flinch, but none of them voiced an argument.

Turning to Jen, she asked, "Can you please give me a ride into Austin? I'll find a motel room there until I can see my brother. Then I'll catch a flight back to New York. At least there, I know I'm dealing with deception, so I'm prepared for it."

Chapter Thirteen

JUAN FELT LIKE he'd been kicked in the gut. He'd tried to warn the team they were making a mistake, but he'd been overruled, and now, she wanted to leave. When he started forward, Sage McCall caught his shirt sleeve in his beefy hand and gave a quick shake of his head.

"Wait. Let Jen help. She may be a wild child at heart, but it's a heart of pure fucking gold—watch and learn." Juan didn't like having his fate in someone else's hands, but the emptiness he'd seen in Lakyn's eyes when she'd looked his way told him he didn't have anything to lose.

"Before you make a decision, let's go down to the gym. When I'm pissed off at the world, I like to vent... sometimes it keeps me from digging myself into a hole I have to ask for help to escape. And damn it all to hell, it frosts my cookies to have to ask the people responsible for my snit for help."

Juan saw Lakyn's shoulders relax marginally as Jen led her from the room. He watched as the two women strolled down the long path toward the onsite training facility, noting Jen had walked right past several motorized carts—smart girl, she was using the distance to buy time. God love her compassionate soul.

"Don't forget, our hot wife worked for the State Department, once a diplomat, always a diplomat. One of the great things about being the second-in-command to a boss who didn't do diddly squat, she learned to negotiate. Hell, by this time tomorrow, she'll have talked her way into renegotiating Lakyn's contracts and the lease on her apartment."

"Sage is right. Tobi loves to take Jen in as a ringer when she is sealing a deal with a new club. Don't get me wrong, Tobi and Gracie built a phenomenally successful business from the ground up, but Jen has helped them refine their skills to the point I expect Wall Street to show up any day, asking the three of them to conduct training seminars." Kyle's smile reflected his pride in his wife's success and his respect for the fact they'd done it on their own. Juan remembered hearing his bosses bragging that Tobi and Gracie had been adamant in their refusal to take any financial help from their husbands.

Turning his attention to Trac, Juan glared at his best friend. "I told you. I fucking told you it was a mistake to leave her out of the loop. You can't play those games with smart women." Looking around the room with pointed looks, Juan waved his arm sweeping them all up in his frustration. "You all have wives who would take you apart if you pulled this shit with them, and yet you set us up for a fall without blinking. Why? Because you wanted to bring Cooper Hicks in without any interference from the one person who cares more about him than anyone else? Fucking hell."

For the first time in his life, Juan Rivera felt like walking away from the career he loved. His family would welcome him with open arms—hell, they' been trying to talk him into joining the family business since they learned he was resigning his commission in the SEALs. Juan was straight up pissed, and he knew better than to say any more or make a decision until he'd cooled down. Turning to walk from the room, Kent West stopped him with a single word.

"Wait." Juan turned to the other man, schooling his expression. "You're right. We fucked up, and we'll set it right, I promise. Trust is essential, and we've betrayed hers and yours." Sitting down on the corner of Kyle's desk, a move he and every other member of the team knew Kyle hated, Kent let one of his long legs swing back and forth. "You know we aren't going to let her leave, right?"

Of course, he knew they'd do everything possible to keep her from leaving, hell, she was in danger and damned well didn't need to be unprotected in Austin or New York. Shifting his frustrated glare from Kent to Kyle, Juan could see the remorse in the other man's expression. Turning to Sam McCall, Juan asked, "What's your wife's favorite flower?"

"Calatheas." Sam answered without hesitation, a flicker of a smile lifting the corners of his mouth.

Turning to Trac, Juan nodded and said, "Take care of it. Weekly. For a year." Trac's brows lifted in surprise, but he didn't argue. Turning back to Kyle, Juan studied his friend and boss closely before shaking his head. "Whatever you're paying Jen isn't enough. Fix it." A slow grin spread across Kent's face before he nodded once, then Juan turned and walked out.

Tomorrow he'd make a healthy donation in her name to a local children's charity he knew Jen favored. Every member of the Prairie Winds team was encouraged to adopt a local charity and many of them supported more than one. The Wests and their parents were believers in giving back, their generosity was just one of the many reasons he respected them.

Walking down the long drive leading to the training

center, Juan was grateful no one had followed him. He needed a few minutes to cool down before he tried to talk to Lakyn. Juan couldn't let her walk away—he had to find a way to fix this mess. His phone vibrated in his pocket, and when he pulled it out, the simple message was from Micah Drake. "Side door." Without questioning the directive, Juan heard the electronic lock disengage as he reached for the handle of the heavy metal door. Walking silently down the hall, Juan could hear Jen's voice encouraging Lakyn to follow through on her punches.

"Make the bag swing. Remember, you're trying to hit the other side, not the one closest to you." More thuds against the bag, then soft laughter. "Much better. I should have had Micah send pictures to the printer, we could have taped them to the bag. That would have been fun, but we probably would have gone through too much paper."

Lakyn's soft laughter was the sweetest sound he'd ever heard—it was so much better than the emotionless speech he'd heard when he'd entered the office less than a half hour ago. Leaning against the wall at the end of the hall where he could see the women's reflections in the glass at the front of the building, he watched as Lakyn vented her frustration on the bag. They were both still wearing their street clothes, and he understood why Jen hadn't wanted to take time to change.

The sheen of sweat reflected on Lakyn's flushed face as she pounded her gloved fists against the heavy bag. Her form might not have been perfect, but she was putting everything she had into each punch. He flinched when she slipped and fell against the bag. Grasping it as is moved slowly away from where she stood, she groaned.

"I'm so out of shape. When the stalking started, I stopped going to the gym because I didn't want to be exposed long enough to walk down the street."

Jen's mouth dropped open as she looked at Lakyn. "Why not take a taxi? I can see not wanting to go if you were worried the stalker was someone at your gym, but why not just call a cab? Holy crap, girl. You have to be making a shit-ton of money, and from the report I read, you don't spend it partying or traveling to all the world's hot spots."

"Taxis are expensive. Why should I pay some driver, who spends most of the three-block trip leering at me in the mirror, twenty bucks?"

Juan was amused at the indignant look on Lakyn's sweat covered face, but the shock reflected on Jen's face made him snort a laugh and quickly step back when she seemed to sense his presence.

"Girl, I don't know about you." The two shared a laugh before sliding to the floor and leaning against the wall facing the windows. God love Jen, she'd made sure he could see Lakyn as they spoke. He listened as Jen tried to explain the rationale behind the decision to keep her brother's visit to the hospital a secret.

"Do you think Cooper has confided in you every time he's been hurt?"

He saw Lakyn's shoulders sag, but he couldn't hear her response.

"If you're going to walk away from Juan and Trac, you need to know they weren't on board with the decision. Juan was particularly adamant you be told, but he was overruled." Jen played with the hem of her shirt while she appeared to be choosing her words carefully. "You're a movie star, have you ever had to play a scene the director's way even though you were sure it was all wrong?"

Lakyn nodded and he fought to stay hidden as Jen

shrugged.

"I've never seen team members stand up to Kyle the way Juan and Trac did. You have to remember, these guys are former military, respect for the chain of command is practically in their DNA. Arguing the way they did was very telling because it was so unusual—not unusual for me... but almost unheard of for the men on the team."

This time Juan saw a small smile play over Lakyn's lips and felt a wave of relief sweep over him.

Jen was amazing. She hadn't told Lakyn to give them another chance, she'd simply given her all the information she needed to make the right choice. He felt his phone vibrate in his pocket again and noticed Jen pull hers out at the same time.

Cooper Hicks will land in Austin in an hour. Transported here immediately thereafter.

Jen held her phone up to show the message to Lakyn. He'd expected her to spring to her feet, but she'd leaned her head back against the wall and closed her eyes.

"I guess I don't have much time to get my temper under control. I'm so pissed at him for not returning my calls or messages. He's never done that, and I've been going insane worrying about him."

What? She hadn't said a word about being angry at her brother. They needed to have a long chat about sharing the things that upset her. Transparency was a large part of the lifestyle and... *Oh my fucking God. Do you even hear yourself? How hypocritical are you?*

Shaking his head as he realized how insane it was to be frustrated with her, Juan stepped around the corner into Lakyn's line of sight. He watched her eyes widen and fill with tears.

"*Cariña*? What's wrong, sweetheart?" Moving slowly to her side, he knelt in front of her and took her hand in his. "Why the tears, beautiful?"

"I'm just mad. I'm totally pissed off, and I don't even know why. Well, that's not really true... it's more like I don't even know where to start. I'm mad as hell at my brother for not answering my calls and messages. Damn it to all to midget goats, he's never done that to me before. I'm furious that a van with masked idiots tried to yank me off the street. I'm mad as hell someone put electronic monitoring equipment in my apartment—fucking hell, that's just creepy. And I'm beyond annoyed no one told me Cooper was hurt... including Cooper. Now, he'll be here before long, and I'm really not in the mood to be nice to him... and no one deserves that kind of greeting." Her shoulders slumped, and she looked like a rapidly deflating balloon.

Pulling her to her feet, he wrapped her in his arms and simply stood with her nestled against his chest for a long time, hoping the simple physical contact would help some of her frustration drain away. It seemed like forever before she finally relaxed in his arms, and once again, he owned a huge debt of gratitude to his sisters for their lessons in the healing power of a hug.

"If you're finished here, let's walk to the cabin and get something to eat before you get ready to greet your brother. I'll bet food and a bubble bath will go a long way to setting you back on track. I know you don't like feeling as though the world around is spinning out of control, but sometimes, you have to just stand very still and let things happen in their own time. Trying to control everything is impossible and exhausting."

"I've tried telling my loving husbands the same thing, but do they listen to me? Oh hell, no. Want to know who's showing them the light? Their daughter... oh yes, indeed. Life at our house is getting more interesting by the day." Jen rose to her feet and gave Lakyn a quick hug.

"Don't be too hard on Cooper, I have a feeling he's already waging a hell of a war with his own guilt. I don't want you to go too easy on him either, but you probably want to save the tar and feathers for another time."

Lakyn gave the other woman a quick hug and thanked her before they set out for the cabin. Juan wasn't surprised to see Trac had already arrived, and he smiled as the other man fell in beside them as they moved down the hall. The frown on Trac's face as they entered the master bathroom made Juan wonder what the hell his friend was thinking. When Lakyn met his glare straight on, Juan wanted to cheer.

Good girl, don't let him intimidate you.

TRAC REACHED FOR Lakyn and pulled her into his arms. "I'm sorry, Princess." The simple words seemed inadequate, but they were all he had to offer. Any excuse he could give would sound as hollow as it would feel, and she deserved better than that from both of the men who'd promised to protect her. At first, he'd been angry at her for challenging the team's decision, then he'd been just as pissed at Juan for reminding everyone he'd seen her reaction coming. He'd disagreed with the Wests' decision, but he'd certainly understood their reasoning.

Realizing he'd let her down had hurt, and he was grateful she hadn't been there to see his initial reaction. One of the things he'd hated the most as a kid was his father's habit of reacting first and thinking later. Trac has sworn he'd never follow in those particular footsteps and damn if he had very nearly made the same mistake.

Fuck me, I know better—that kind of damage would have completely undermined the trust we were just beginning to build.

Juan looked on for several minutes, then nodded to the door. "I'm going to shower in the guest suite, then make us something to eat. Don't be too long." Trac was grateful for the time alone with their sweet sub, it was a gift, and he appreciated Juan's understanding.

"Come on, Princess, let's shower and find out what Juan's making to eat. He's an amazing cook, so we don't want to miss out." He helped her out of her clothes before stripping out of his own and leading her into the hot shower.

Trac let his hands speak for him. He was careful to keep his touch tender but not sexual, this was about relaxation, not arousal. By the time he finished, her muscles were pliant beneath his fingertips, and her eyes had lost some of the wariness he'd seen when the three of them first returned to the cabin.

Moving her to the other end of the shower, Trac positioned one of the side-mounted shower heads so it pulsed hot water between her shoulder blades. Her soft groan as the pulsing water continued to massage her back sent a surge of blood to his cock, and he fought the urge to push her against the wall and lose himself in her softness.

Fucking hell, he couldn't even remember the last time he'd taken a shower with a woman without giving her at least one orgasm. As much as he thought she'd benefit from a release or two, she needed time to eat and settle a bit before her brother hit the door. Cam's description of

Cooper's injuries listed a litany of superficial wounds that would look much worse than they actually were, so Lakyn needed as much fortification as possible.

Finishing his own shower quickly, he shut off the water and led her out of the large enclosure. It didn't take them long to dress and make their way to the kitchen where Juan was already hard at work. When Trac saw her eyes widen in surprise, he leaned down close.

"This is what happens when you're the youngest in a large family and all your siblings are female," he whispered. "They were determined their little brother was going to be the catch of the century."

Lakyn sniffed the air, and Trac heard her stomach growl. He'd no sooner seated her at the table than Juan set a sizzling tray of meat and vegetables on the table between the three place settings. Lakyn's sweet groan as she sniffed the air sent another rush of blood to his cock, and Trac had to fight the urge to shift the damned thing away from the zipper of his jeans. At this rate, he was going to have to take another shower—a very *cold* shower before meeting her brother. *Damn.*

Chapter Fourteen

COOPER LOOKED OUT the tinted windows of the car before turning his attention back to Kyle West. "I didn't expect the VIP treatment—I could have rented a car."

"You could have, but that's not the way things work in Texas. We treat our guests better than that, and God forbid if Lilly West got wind one of her sons hadn't greeted a guest properly." Cooper suspected the man was only half teasing. He'd heard stories about the West matriarch, but he'd never met her. Kyle must have sensed the direction his mind was headed because he grinned and shook his head. "Don't worry, you'll meet her soon enough, and yes, she's every inch the wildcard you've heard about."

Copper wasn't sure it was possible for Lilly West to live up to her reputation, but he would reserve judgment.

"Where is Lakyn?" He'd never had to face his sister looking like he'd had his ass handed to him, and the truth was, he wasn't looking forward to it. If Cam had still been headquartered in Houston, Cooper would have detoured there until he'd healed enough he wouldn't scare his sister spitless.

"She's staying in one of the cabins behind the club." He and Kyle had only worked together a few times, but Cooper knew people well enough to know when he hadn't gotten the whole story. Waiting for the other man to elaborate seemed to be taking an awfully long time, but he was determined to wait out the uncomfortable silence. Kyle finally chuckled as he turned onto what looked like a long drive.

"Damn, I don't know why I didn't send Kent to pick you up." When they parked in front of the club, Cooper raised a brow in question. Why hadn't Kyle taken him the cabin where Lakyn was staying? Kyle shut off the car but didn't get out. Turning in his seat, the other man studied him for several seconds before speaking.

"I don't have a sister, so I'm in unfamiliar territory here. I didn't take you to the cabin where Lakyn is staying because she isn't alone. She is with two members of the team."

"Are they her bodyguards?" Cooper wasn't naïve, and Kyle's obvious discomfort was a dead giveaway, but he'd be damned if he was going to make it easy on the man whose reputation as unflappable was practically a legend among SEALs.

"Not really although I can assure you anyone wanting to get to her is going to have to go through them, particularly after the disaster on the river."

Yeah, Cam had already briefed him on the close call she'd had in New York and the second fiasco right under the Prairie Winds teams' nose. Heads were going to roll when he found out who was targeting his sister.

"Juan Rivera and Trac Hughes are both Doms although Juan isn't as committed to the lifestyle as Trac. I'll let them speak for themselves about their intentions, but I can tell you they are both honorable. You can believe anything they tell you."

Cooper considered Kyle's words and was surprised at the relief he felt, knowing Lakyn had finally met someone who would look out for her. If Kyle vouched for them, the men were obviously stand up guys, but he'd need to meet them and decide for himself.

"Two? Jesus, man, what's in the water down here? Remind me to drink juice."

"Brother," Kyle laughed and shook his head, "you look like you need something a lot stronger than juice. We'll get you settled in one of the rooms above the club before hitting the bar. When is the last time you ate?"

"Catalina had a sandwich and chips waiting for me when I got out of the hospital, but I slept on the plane, so I haven't eaten anything since then."

"Catalina Adler?" When Cooper nodded, Kyle smiled and shook his head. "Damn I'd love to recruit her, but I'm not sure she and Jen could be corralled… Hell, I'm not sure the world is ready for that combination yet." Cooper grabbed his small bag and followed Kyle into the large building wondering who Jen was, and why she and Catalina would be a threat.

Seriously? What the hell am I thinking? Cat's a threat on a good day.

LAKYN WAS GETTING tired of watching Juan and Trac try to stealthily check their phones. Whoever was updating them wasn't sharing the information with her, and she was silently fuming. They'd finished dinner, and she was about to go upstairs to change when she caught Juan, once again, slipping his phone from his pocket. Stalking over closer, she stood with her hands on her hips and glared up at him.

"I want to know what's going on. I'm tired of being left out of the damned loop. Is my brother going to show up or not? Damn this is fucking annoying." She'd no sooner finished speaking than she heard both men snarl something about language and a heartbeat later she was over Juan's shoulder being carried up the stairs like a sack of potatoes. "What the fuck? Put me down." A sharp slap on her ass made her freeze for a second before she started kicking.

"Stop, *Cariña*. You are already in enough trouble for your attitude and language. Do not compound the problem by adding careless behavior to your list of offenses, or you won't sit comfortably for a week."

Offenses? What the ever-loving hell? She opened her mouth to protest but saw Trac glaring at her as they moved down the hall.

"Don't. Just don't. We've been more than patient with you, but you agreed to be our submissive and it's time you understood what that looks like. And it certainly doesn't look like you copping an attitude and cursing like a sailor." Trac's word annoyed her, but she also realized he *probably* wasn't wrong. Juan set her on her feet beside the bed but didn't take his hands off her.

"Do we curse at you, *Cariña*?" Now that she thought about it, they'd never raised their voices or cursed at her. Shaking her head, Lakyn saw Juan's expression darken and remembered she was supposed to answer with words.

"No, but I'm tired of being left out of things that pertain to me. It's annoying as he... ck." She'd been taking care of herself for a long time and not knowing what was going on made her edgy.

"We'll always tell you everything you need to know. Part of your role as our submissive is to trust us to keep you apprised of anything important related to your safety, career, friends, or brother." Trac's voice was all business, but she could see the warmth in his eyes.

"Keep in mind, *Cariña*, what we consider significant may not always be in line with what you consider important." The man who had previously been her suave Latin lover was now standing in front of her with his arms crossed over his muscular chest looking every inch as intimidating as Trac. "I'm afraid I've given you the wrong impression, Lakyn. It seems you believe you can run over me because I've allowed you a lot of latitude. Just because I don't take a hard line with D/s protocol doesn't mean I'll allow you to be disrespectful. When you disrespect me, you are undermining your own trust in me as your Dom, and if I allowed it, I'd be teaching you that you can't trust me when the chips are down—and my darling, *Cariña,* that is simply not the case."

It took her mind a few seconds to catch up with what Juan had said, and she had to admit she understood his reasoning. She didn't respond because he hadn't asked her a question, but he'd evidently seen the understanding dawn in her expression because he nodded once as if to say it was time to proceed.

"Strip."

Lakyn blinked in surprise, unsure for a few seconds she'd heard him right. He wanted her to take off all of her clothes? Standing right here in front of him? Seriously? When she didn't immediately respond, Juan frowned.

"What part of my command is confusing, *Cariña*?"

Taking a deep breath, she reached for the hem of the t-shirt she'd put on after her shower. Pulling it slowly over her head, she felt her nipples tighten into stiff peaks at his blatant stare. His pointed look at her yoga pants was a clear indication he was getting tired of waiting, and Lakyn saw stalling wasn't going to work to her advantage, so she tucked her thumbs in the waistband and skimmed the form-fitting pants down her legs, leaving them on the floor.

"When we tell you to strip, we'll expect you to fold your clothing neatly and hand it to us."

It took her a few seconds to register his instructions, and when she bent to retrieve her shirt and pants from the floor, she couldn't help but notice his erection straining against the zipper of his faded jeans. The evidence of his attraction was oddly empowering. It was good to know she affected him in a way that wasn't steeped in frustration.

She started to hand the folded clothes to Juan but Trac stepped forward, taking them from her while Juan sat on the edge of the bed. When he wrapped his large hand around her wrist, he didn't give her time to wonder what he planned. With a swift pull, Lakyn found herself draped over his lap with her ass peaked high enough, she knew her bare and very wet pussy was displayed for the entire world to see. Her hands were moving over the smooth wooden surface of the bedroom floor, trying to find a comfortable position to brace herself when, without warning, the first swat seared her right ass cheek.

Holy fucking hellions!

JUAN KNEW LAKYN hadn't been ready for the first swat—she gasped and gave a startled yelp but hadn't said anything. He watched as the imprint of his hand bloomed a nice shade of pink over her creamy skin.

"I'm starting out easy, but I intend for this to be a lesson, so we'll ramp things up quickly. What's your safe word, Lakyn?"

"Easy? Oh, my fucking God." Juan rolled his eyes at her response and looked at Trac who was standing to the side, shaking his head. Giving her another swat, this one more intense than the first one, Juan repeated the question along with a warning about her language.

"I asked your safe word. Don't add to your punishment by continuing to curse, *Cariña*. You are better than this." Cleaning up her language was going to be one of his priorities with her, she was much too talented and beautiful to sully it by talking like a drunken nineteen-year-old.

"Red."

Her one-word answer made him smile. The little minx still hadn't put herself in their care. She may have physically submitted, but her mind was still holding the reins of control in her tight grip. He didn't challenge her for an explanation because it would only give her more time to build another wall they'd need to tear down.

"Use it if you need to, *Cariña*." Giving her several solid swats without ever striking the same place twice, Juan watched as her ass turned a lovely shade of pink before the deeper shades of rose appeared. He was pleased she hadn't noticed the mirror behind her, and he smiled when Trac stepped to the side, so Juan could see how wet her pretty pussy was becoming.

"I'm not sure we're using the right punishment for our mouthy little sub. It seems like she is enjoying her punishment a little more than she should." Trac stepped closer and slid his fingers through her wet folds. Juan smiled when her legs parted, and her back arched.

"I see what you mean. Our sub is soaking wet, I'm not sure this spanking is going to get the message across. Let's up the stakes, shall we?" While Juan repositioned Lakyn over the edge of the bed with her legs spread wide, Trac retrieved the plug and lube they'd planned to use when they took Lakyn to the club later tonight. Now, as part of her punishment, she'd get to wear the plug while she reunited with her brother. Perhaps the challenge of maintaining control while chatting with Cooper would help her remember to clean up her language in the future.

"Reach back and spread your cheeks, Princess." Trac took the lead and Juan stepped back to enjoy the show. It was going to be fun to watch the tortured look on his friend's face when he pushed into her heated flesh once he had the plug firmly in place. Her face flamed with embarrassment, and when she attempted to hide by burying her face in the soft quilt covering the bed, Trac gave her heated ass a sharp slap.

"Do not hide your face from us, Lakyn. It's important we are able to read your body's signals and being able to see into those stunning eyes is a large part of that."

As Trac drizzled the cool lube at the top of her ass, Juan grinned at her gasp.

"When you're a good girl, we'll warm the lube for you, *Cariña*, but when you're naughty, you won't get those special considerations." He and Trac both knew it would have been easy to use her body's own honey as lube, God knew she was wet enough, but where would the fun be in that?

"This isn't a large plug, but it has a couple of special features I think you'll find make up for its diminutive size." Juan wanted to laugh out loud at his friend's comment—there was a reason the team referred to Trac as the King of Understatements. The plug he was slowly fucking deeper and deeper into her pretty rosette was going to light her up like the New York skyline on Independence Day.

Chapter Fifteen

TRAC WATCHED THE plug stretch Lakyn's pretty rosette as he pushed it fractionally deeper with each thrust. Her soft moans and delicious sighs were making him so damned hard, his cock throbbed against the metal zipper of his jeans. Fuck, he was going to have a permanent zipper tattoo if he wasn't careful.

"You're doing great, Princess. Push back when you feel me pushing forward, then relax those muscles. Submission is a journey, not a destination."

A fresh wave of moisture coated her sex, and the scent of her arousal filled the air around them. Once the plug was firmly seated in her ass, Trac smoothed his palms down Lakyn's sides from just below her breasts to her hips. They gave their lovely sub a few minutes to settle before Trac pulled her to her feet. Juan stripped out of his clothes and moved into place.

Before turning her to face Juan, Trac used the pads of his fingers to lift her chin so he could look into her eyes. Moving his thumb back and forth over her plump lower lip, he watched as the variations in the color of her eyes darkened in proportion to the desire so clearly reflected in them. The outer ring of her iris was a deep shade of amethyst, and without question, the most beautiful and unique eye color he'd ever seen.

"You're going to use this pretty mouth to pleasure

your other Master while I fuck you." Her face flushed a lovely shade of deep pink and he wanted to remind her there was no reason to be embarrassed, but that was a discussion they could have later. "We're going to play a game, Princess. If you can make Master Juan come before I make you come, you'll get to pick which dress you wear to the club this evening, but if you fail, we'll choose for you. He wanted to smile at the fire he saw in her eyes. Evidently, their sub had a competitive spirit. Trac could tell her she was being set up to fail, but why ruin the fun?

"I'll even give you a head start while I strip. Turning her toward Juan, he watched as she didn't waste any time getting into position before flicking the tip of her pink tongue along the stiff outer ring circling the head of his friend's cock. Juan's head fell back on his shoulders as his eyes closed. Without opening his eyes, Juan gave Trac the hand signal for *hurry,* making him bite back a smile. Juan Rivera was usually the epitome of control—making sure the woman he was topping had at least two orgasms before he let himself go. Hell, Trac had seen Juan make love to a woman for hours before finally letting himself come.

When Juan's eyes opened in narrow slits, he leveled Trac with a look of impatience. Shaking himself out of the stupor he'd been caught in, Trac shed his clothing quickly and tore open the condom package he'd already set on the small table. After sheathing himself, Trac reached for the small remote that was going to tip the odds so far in their favor, Lakyn wasn't going to stand a snowball's chance in hell of winning the challenge.

Circling the tip of his cock in her cream, Trac teased Lakyn's opening until she was pushing back, trying to force him inside. Slapping her ass twice before reaching around, giving both nipples a sharp pinch.

Chapter Sixteen

COOPER WATCHED TRAC Hughes and Juan Rivera escort his kid sister out of the room, fighting the urge to tell them to keep their bloody paws to themselves. With a flash of insight, Cooper realized Lakyn was no longer a little girl. The white-hot lance of pain piercing his heart at the loss was sharper than the discomfort he felt at his sharp intake of breath. The fucker who broke his ribs would pay someday; the world was a big place, but hired thugs tended to show up time and again.

"They'll take good care of her. They've been looking for a woman to share for a long time." Cooper turned to look at Kent West and cocked his brow.

"Does everybody here share their women because I've never been very good at sharing my toys." The flash of fire in Kent's eyes told Cooper his words had hit their mark.

"Our wife isn't a toy although I'll admit I like playing with her. When you meet her, you'll do well to curb that attitude, or she'll take you apart, and no one here will help you. She'll also serve your manhood up to you on a silver platter if you make that insinuation about your sister. They're friends, and Tobi protects her friends as fiercely as she does her family."

Cooper hadn't met the infamous Tobi West, but he'd heard about her, and he looked forward to it. She'd befriended his sister without knowing Lakyn Hicks was also Lakyn Storm, and she hadn't walked away when she'd learned her internet pal was, in fact, an international celebrity. Cooper had always been equally baffled by the number of people in Lakyn's life who were there because she was famous as he was by those who walked away because she was too much trouble to be friends with.

Leveling a look at Kent, he knew it was time to clear up the other man's misunderstanding before things became any more strained between them.

"I'm looking forward to meeting Tobi. I've heard a lot about her, and she has already earned my respect simply by befriending Lakyn. I assure you, I'll never give her any cause to think I don't respect her or my sister. Keep in mind, the woman who just walked out of this room holds my heart in the palm of her hand." He ran his bruised fingers through his shaggy hair and sighed.

"Knowing someone is targeting Lakyn because of me is tearing me apart with worry, and I'll happily kill whoever is behind this and never lose a moments sleep over it." It was the God's honest truth. If he lived a hundred lifetimes, Cooper didn't think he'd be able to make up for the things he'd done. It didn't matter that he'd been acting in the name of justice or on the orders of the United States government—each of those acts was a mark against his soul.

Kent nodded and smiled. "Tobi loves loud, and she loves large. She has a heart the size of Texas and is exactly what she appears to be—there is nothing remotely phony about her. But you don't ever want to underestimate her ability to slice and dice you if she thinks you aren't treating one of *hers* right. And just to be sure there are no questions, she considers everybody remotely associated with the club or our teams to be hers.

storm, not the fucking wind itself. There was a very real irony in Juan and Trac finding her huddled in a damned dust storm; sometimes, fate had a strange sense of humor.

"Does she know about the chip?" And there it was— the confirmation he'd known was coming but had dreaded hearing. Micah's voice hadn't carried any judgment, he'd simply asked a question Cooper was embarrassed to say he hadn't even considered as a possibility.

"Hell, I didn't figure it out until a few minutes ago. I should have, but I was so far past exhaustion when I hit your gates, I was barely functioning." Cooper had slept for almost twenty hours, more rest than he usually got in a week. "It's the only explanation of how that prick knew she was on the tube." Micah nodded as he pushed away from the wall and moved closer to the window.

"We knew as soon as Trac and Juan drove through the gate with her. They're aware and have looked—well, hell." Cooper smiled at the other man's unease.

"It's okay, Micah, I already know about Juan and Trac's interest in Lakyn. As long as they treat her well and protect her, I won't have a problem with their lifestyle. My sister is strong enough to say no, and it would be damned hypocritical of me to criticize her interest in dominance and submission when I'm a Dom. I've suspected she was a submissive, but she hadn't shown any recognition until recently." Sighing and running a hand through his shaggy hair, Cooper looked at Kyle and hoped his smile reached his eyes.

"To be honest, I was damned suspicious when I learned the Wests' wife had befriended my sister. Seriously, what are the odds of the two of them randomly finding each other on the internet? I swear that girl has been giving me ulcers since the day my parents brought her home."

Unfortunately, he'd been the only one interested in Lakyn's well-being until she landed her first modeling contract. Their parents had blatantly exploited their only daughter, and Cooper shuddered each time he considered how much of her money they'd squandered before he'd threatened to contact the authorities.

Kyle and Kent both chuckled and assured him they'd had similar misgivings when they'd learned the women had been corresponding. Ordinarily, Cooper didn't believe in coincidences, but this situation was turning out to be anything but average. Overall, the discussion had gone a long way to clear the air, and Cooper was grateful when all three men assured him if he joined their team, Lakyn would be protected as well. He hadn't talked to Juan or Trac about their long-term plans, but he suspected his younger sister was going to have more protection than she wanted.

"She had an emergency appendectomy several years ago. I assume that's when the tracker was inserted. I'd just started with the Agency, and Cam stayed with her after the surgery until I could get there." Fucking hell, Lakyn was going to go ballistic when she learned his career had cast such a long shadow over her life. He had no idea how he was going to tell her, but he wasn't going to shove the burden onto anyone else's shoulders.

Returning his attention to the men on the other side of the window, Cooper shook his head when Parker Andrews threatened to shove Cox's ass out the front door and let the vultures have him if he didn't start talking. Cox leaned back in his chair, his legs stretched out in front of him, and crossed his beefy arms over his chest, the man's confidence unshaken by the Police Chief's threat.

Parker pulled his phone from his pocket, a grin spreading across his face as he studied the screen. When the Chief stood and moved to the door, Cox sat up in his chair. For the first time since the interview started, Cox looked uncomfortable, and Cooper almost laughed out loud when Cameron Barnes stepped into the room. Cooper heard Kent West chuckle beside him.

"Bet you twenty he just pissed his pants."

"Jesus, you're as bad as Tobi, I swear I'd send the two of you to finishing school if I wasn't afraid of the lawsuit that would follow." Kyle's words might have been critical, but amusement danced in his eyes. Cooper felt himself beginning to relax for the first time in months.

"Well, he obviously knew who Cam was—hell, did you see how he paled? He's fucking white as a sheet. It does my heart good to see terror in his eyes."

"Call it a preview of coming attractions." Cooper hadn't meant to say the words aloud but when the other men in the room howled with laughter, he was reminded he was dealing with a group of former Special Forces operatives who didn't miss anything. Parker joined them a few minutes later, leaving Cox with Cam—*yes, indeed, things are about to get interesting*.

"It's probably a violation of some ethics clause to leave the son of a bitch with Cam, but in my opinion, Cox signed his life away the minute he accepted the job." Parker turned up the volume of the audio system, and they listened as Cameron Barnes worked his magic.

"Your decision to harm the younger sister of a CIA operative was a critical error—one I can assure you was not worth whatever paltry sum you were paid." Cam sat forward in his chair, leaning his forearms on his thighs, and sighed. "You need to make a very important decision, Mr. Cox. You need to decide whose life you value more. Yours?

Or the person who hired you? I'm quite sure your handler didn't mention Lakyn Storm's connection to Cooper Hicks and probably didn't mention the young woman is also a personal friend of mine and under the protection of the Prairie Winds team of contract Special Operatives. Long story, short—they threw you to the wolves, Mr. Cox, and all of those beasts are nipping at your heels."

Cooper wanted to laugh at the ashen look on James Cox's face. Cam hadn't raised his voice, he'd simply outlined the situation with unerring accuracy. What Cam hadn't mentioned was he'd already gotten a call from the Agency to bring Cox in—somebody in D.C. wanted their hands on the man sitting in the next room, and Cooper wanted a name.

Chapter Eighteen

L AKYN DISCONNECTED THE call and shook her head in disbelief. She'd never been called back for a re-shoot a month later. She couldn't even ask Reggie what was going on because he'd been MIA since Cooper showed up—and Lakyn didn't believe for a second *that* was a coincidence. She'd asked Cooper, Trac, and Juan several times over the past few days if any of them had spoken with her manager, and they'd all insisted they hadn't talked to him, but she still had the nagging feeling she wasn't being told the truth.

"What's wrong, *Cariña?*" Juan was already walking toward her, his eyes darkened with concern. "You look worried and confused." She recounted the odd phone call she'd just gotten from one of the smaller fashion houses she worked with and wasn't surprised to see the questions in his eyes.

"It's very unusual… actually, this is the first time I've been called back this long after a session. Most photographers and agencies are on a very tight timeline, so they can't wait this long for a re-shoot. They also know models are continually traveling, so asking one to return for a re-shoot more than a day or two after a session is unheard of." She'd barely finished speaking when she noticed Trac at the other side of the room with his phone pressed to his ear.

Juan was silent for so long, Lakyn was beginning to worry he was joining the ranks of those people who had decided she was more trouble than she was worth. It was always painful when friends walked out of her life, but she had the feeling it would be soul-crushing this time.

You knew it wouldn't last... no one stays forever, even Cooper disappears for months on end. Stop whining and deal.

Tilting his head to the side, Juan studied her so closely she was starting to feel like a science experiment.

"What didn't you think would last, *Cariña?*" Damn it, when was she going to learn to keep her mouth shut, so her thoughts didn't tumble out? "Did you think we'd abandon you the first-time things didn't go exactly as planned?"

"That's exactly what she thought because it's happened before, hasn't it? Princess, we need to talk. I believe we've done you a great disservice. Juan and I have been waiting until we'd had more time to establish trust between us to broach this subject, but now I'd have to say that was a mistake."

Lakyn was still reeling from the realization she'd spoken her disappointment aloud that she was having trouble tracking Trac's comments, and since he hadn't asked her a question, she decided to err on the side of the angels and stay quiet. They must have known why she hadn't responded because they both smiled.

"*Cariña,* this is a discussion between lovers, not a D/s scene, so please don't hesitate to speak. We want you to feel comfortable with us, no matter the situation. If you can trust us with your body and your pleasure, you can surely trust us with your questions and comments."

"As long as you are respectful, we'll always be open to hearing what you have to say. Remember, we don't speak disrespectfully to you, and we expect the same in return."

Trac was right, they'd never spoken harshly to her, and

now, she regretted the lack of respect she'd shown them. When she thought back over the time since they'd met, she was embarrassed to admit they'd treated her much better than her behavior warranted. Good grief, when had she become such a diva who didn't treat others with common courtesy?

"I don't know what to say except you're right. So many people have walked away, I've come to expect it. Cooper has gone above and beyond, I don't want to give anyone the impression I'm not grateful... because I am. His job took him out of the country so often and for such extended periods of time, I often laid awake wondering if I'd ever see him again. The prospect of being truly alone in this world was terrifying." When Juan started to speak, she held up her hand, wanting to finish before she lost her nerve.

"My career seems glamorous to those on the outside, but I assure you, it is anything but. I've been toying with the idea of starting my own fashion line in the future, but..." When she faltered, Juan stepped closer and lifted her chin, so her gaze met his.

"*Cariña*, if there is one thing Trac and I learned while we were in the military it was how short life can be." He brushed a stray strand of her hair back over her shoulder and smiled.

"My grandmother always reminded us that we should never delay joy. I'm not sure I truly understood what she was talking about until her memorial service, listening to her friends and family recount all their memories of her spontaneous moments of laughter and what she called *shenanigans*. As I sat there, I realized not one person talked about the time she spent working, they only spoke of all the wonderful memories they had of her fun-loving spirit and wise counsel." By the time he'd finished speaking,

Lakyn felt tears streaming down her cheeks.

"It's very humbling to know I've spent so much of my life focused on nothing but work. Before the great tubing caper, I hadn't done anything just for the fun of it since I first started modeling as a child. Everything has always been about working and making money... money that would *someday* fund my lifelong dream of designing clothing and accessories." Trac joined them and gave her a rueful smile.

"Juan's right, you know, life is brutally short and working yourself into an early grave is no way to spend the time you've been given." Leaning forward, he pressed a quick kiss to her forehead, and his masculine scent washed over her, a stark reminder there was more to life than running from one job to the next. "Let us accompany you to New York. You need the protection and help with management, and we're capable and willing."

"And we won't care if you use us for sex—that's got to count for something." Juan's teasing words made her laugh, and she was grateful for the change in the mood surrounding them. *What could be better than hot guys to keep me safe who are even better in bed?* If it was so perfect, why did she feel as if something was missing? Chastising herself for seeing the glass as half full, Lakyn quickly thanked them, and the three of them began making travel plans.

Chapter Nineteen

C OOPER STOOD ALONGSIDE the stone fireplace in the
Wests office, staring at his sister, certain she'd lost her
ever-loving mind. He'd listened as she detailed the reasons
she felt the callback she'd gotten was out of the ordinary,
and he understood her reasoning. What he didn't understand was why she'd go back when she knew it was likely a
set-up.

Knowing Trac Hughes and Juan Rivera were planning
to return with her was only a small comfort. Cooper's
reservation was the men's close relationship with Lakyn.
He knew as well as anyone how easy it was to become
distracted by a woman you were charged with protecting—
or one you were supposed to be shadowing to gather
information rather than fucking on every available horizontal surface.

"Hey, big brother, I recognize that glazed over look.
You're totally zoned out. Holy hand bells, you aren't
listening to anything I'm saying. Drat, that's flipping
annoying. Just so you know, I'm not asking your permission. I'm simply playing nice and giving you a heads up
that I have to leave for a while."

Fuck. She was right—about zoning out at least, but he
had heard her every word. As a Navy SEAL, Cooper had
already been good at active listening while dividing his
attention and sorting through a related problem, but his

Agency training had ramped that up several notches. It seemed he had a natural affinity for functioning on several levels at one time, and the only person who *always* called him out on it was his little sister—*and isn't that too fucking humbling for words.*

"I didn't zone out. Just because I don't agree with you doesn't mean I'm not listening. Hell, I'm damned impressed Trac and Juan seem to have made some progress in improving your language. Your mouth has been writing checks your ass couldn't cash for a long time, sweet cheeks." It was a dirty trick, and Cooper had to admit, he felt a twinge of regret when he saw embarrassment flash in her eye, followed by a moment's annoyance—or was that pain? He hadn't meant to hurt her feelings, but he did want to set her back a bit. She wasn't taking her safety as seriously as she needed to, and he wasn't at all pleased with her nonchalant attitude.

Lakyn had always underestimated the risks his job posed to her, and that was partly his fault. He'd never leveled with her about the kind of work he'd been doing for the past several years. She might not have known the specifics of missions when he was a SEAL, but there was enough information available, she hadn't been completely clueless either. Cooper had expected Lakyn to gather her anger around her like a cloak and fire back at him—what he hadn't expected was the petite blonde he'd seen walk by the open doorway to back up. She stood staring at him, her hands on her hips, her lips firmed into a line, fire blazing from her eyes.

"You're in for it now." Kent's low chuckle came from his left, but a quick glance at Kyle let Cooper know he evidently hadn't seen the tiny avenging angel. Her gaze moved from him to his sister, then back to him, and

Cooper would have sworn she grew two inches taller as she took in Lakyn's expression. She zeroed in on him and stalked forward.

"Who are you? What makes you think you can speak to one our guests like that? Didn't your mama teach you it's rude to embarrass people in front of their friends? I don't think I like you very much."

Cooper fought his grin at the small fireball's understatement. She must have seen the amusement in his eyes because she tapped the toe of her stilettos and glared.

"Boy, oh boy, guys like you frost my cookies. From the looks of you, I'm not the only one who thinks you're an ill-mannered ass."

"Kitten, you know you are *not* supposed to interrupt meetings." Kyle's words were probably intended to sound menacing, but the laughter in his voice had ruined the effect.

"If it's not a public forum, you should close the door. I was just walking down the hall, minding my own business when this butt-muffin started blowing mean words at Lakyn." Her face paled and she clasped her hand over her heart so dramatically, Cooper dropped his arms and started to step forward, but Kent's hand on his shoulder stilled him.

"Oh, fudge nuggets, I sound like one of those Stepford mommies in the kids' library group. Damn it all to dangling doo-dads, look what you made me do. This is all your fault." She pointed a long scarlet red fingernail at him before shaking her head. Turning on her heel, the diminutive blonde tornado pulled Lakyn to her feet giving her a fierce hug.

"You come out to the kitchen when you're done, okay? And don't you dare take any trash from that guy. You stick with Juan and Trac, they won't treat you ugly like that yo-yo." Without looking back at him, she walked out of the room with her head held high. She pulled the door closed behind her, and the quiet snick of the latch was followed by an uproar of laughter from the men in the room.

Kent looked at him, shaking his head. "Don't say I didn't warn you."

"As I'm sure you have already figured out, Cooper, that was our wife and our submissive, though she seems incapable of mastering the finer points of submission." Kyle's voice held more amusement than annoyance. Cooper looked around the room to see several of the men battling to contain their laughter and suspected what he'd just experienced was a small initiation of sorts. His reaction would determine how the Wests and every member of their team viewed him.

"Well, she's right." Turning to Lakyn, he smiled at the only person in the world who truly meant anything to him. She'd taught him the meaning of unconditional love the moment he held her in his arms as a child. Even at ten years old, he'd known there wasn't anything he wouldn't do for her.

"Lakyn, I apologize. You hold my heart in your hand, and I'm grateful you have a friend who was willing to confront a stranger—at the risk of making her husbands angry—to defend you. Hold on tight to that friendship, sweet cheeks because I can tell you from experience, that kind of loyalty is damned hard to come by."

He'd deliberately repeated the nickname he'd given her when she first started modeling in hopes he could begin erasing the damage he'd done by using it in a *diss* a few minutes earlier. If he was going to build the new life he'd dreamed of—one where he felt connected to the people he worked and played with—he needed to maneuver his way out of the quagmire he'd created.

Hell, not so long ago, he'd growled at Cat Adler for the same damned thing.

Yes, indeed your life is officially a shit show when you're comparing yourself to the one woman who drives you fucking insane.

Chapter Twenty

LAKYN WANTED TO snatch Trac bald. Had there ever been a human more annoying? He was taking the bodyguard thing to a whole new level of ridiculous. Knowing Cooper approved was proof enough the whole thing was out of control. Hell, she'd barely been able to go to the bathroom alone. Juan was staying busy, acting as her manager, so he hadn't been available to act as a mediator, something he'd easily managed until they'd returned to New York.

Walking down the street to the studio where the re-shoot was scheduled, Lakyn noticed there were several dark sedans with tinted windows parked along the street. The morning sun was bright despite the shadows from the skyscrapers, and she was grateful for the added anonymity of her dark glasses and wide-brimmed hat. She wasn't sure if they were friends of the men flanking her or not, and before she could ask, Lakyn saw Trac tap the earpiece he was wearing.

"All clear?" He'd spoken so softly, she had barely heard him, but evidently whoever was on the other end had because he seemed to relax, at least marginally, as they entered the building. She hadn't been to this particular studio before, so she took her time walking through the large lobby, enjoying the architectural details and crafts-manship of a bygone era.

The small cream and black octagon tiles had been laid in an intricate sunburst pattern that wouldn't be nearly as impressive with today's technology. Knowing the craftsmen who built this building designed and built it without that advantage was remarkable. The bronze angel faces featured along crown molding made her wonder what the building's original purpose had been. As if he'd read her mind, Juan looked down at her and smiled as they entered the elevator.

"It's remarkable, isn't it? I've always enjoyed period architecture, the meanings behind various elements because they are often so different from what they seem. The various pediments, dentil ornamentations, finials, and medallions—so many of them are deeply entrenched in history."

Lakyn was astonished to find out he had such a keen interest in the beauty surrounding them. Most people walked into and by amazing buildings every day without giving them a second glance. Lakyn often found herself walking into things because she was always looking up, fascinated with the intricate details most people ignored.

Trac hadn't said anything, but she'd seen his lips twitch while Juan had been speaking. She started forward when the doors of the elevator slid open, but Juan wrapped his hand around her upper arm holding her back as Trac stepped into the dimly lit hall. The lobby had been filled with light, so it seemed odd this floor was so poorly illuminated.

"Don't move. The building was cleared, but something isn't right."

"I don't hear anything. Usually, I can hear the chatter of my agency's make-up and hair team. Did they confirm with you?" When he nodded, she frowned. "Then they must be here." The next thing she heard was Trac shouting from the distance for them to go before the hallway exploded in a ball of fire.

TRAC NOTICED THE trip wire the minute he stepped off the elevator. He'd easily stepped over it and the next two but hadn't seen the security camera above him pivot until he was already pushing open the heavy metal door to the stairwell.

Shouting over his shoulder at Juan to get Lakyn out, he jumped down the first set of steps, easily landing on his feet, but the explosion above him blew the door to the hall onto the stairs. The damned door was well made and slid quickly down the stairs knocking his feet out from under him. When his ass hit the horizontal surface of the door, it was enough weight shift to send him sledding down the next set of stairs, slamming him into the concrete wall.

Fucking hell, his ears were ringing like a son of a bitch from the explosion, and now his vision blurred from the blow he'd taken when his head collided with the wall. Staggering to his feet, he could hear a door several floors down slam open. The muffled sound of boots running up the stairs was the last thing he remembered before darkness closed in around him.

COOPER HICKS WAS watching the monitor in a nearby van when he saw a glint of light along a narrow wire picked up by Trac Hughes body cam. He knew instantly what the other man was facing and was already sprinting across the street when he heard Hughes shout, "Go. Go. Go" to Juan and Lakyn. Kent's voice came over his earpiece, telling the team Lakyn and Juan were still descending, so he hit the door to the stairwell at a full run, slamming the door against the wall and taking the stairs two and three at a time.

His heart skipped a beat when he found Hughes slumped to the floor, but a quick check of his pulse showed he was alive. The damned man was huge, carrying his dead-weight down three floors was going to be a bitch, but Cooper wasn't going to take a chance waiting for the fire department to arrive. Calling for back-up, he lifted one of the men his sister was so damned fond of over his shoulder and started down the stairs. Christ, his broken ribs were already throbbing, and he'd only managed to go down two flights of stairs.

Leaning against the wall, trying to catch his breath, Cooper heard Hughes shout, "Put me down, asshole, before you puncture a fucking lung." He would have laughed out loud as he set the man on his feet if it wouldn't have hurt so much.

"Wait here, help is on the way." He took in Trac's appearance and wondered how he'd gotten the big goose egg on his forehead. "Where are you hurt?"

"What?"

Cooper tried not to smile at Trac's shout. *Okay, safe to say his hearing took a hit.* Cooper had been close to enough explosions to know how annoying the ringing was and how damned long it lasted. Hopefully, Trac's concussion wasn't so severe, they couldn't give him something to knock his ass out because the only thing Cooper had ever found to help him escape the annoying sound was sleep.

Kent ran up beside them and gave him a questioning look. "Is there some reason you two are standing in the stairwell of a burning building, shooting the shit?"

"What?"

This time Cooper did laugh, then held his ribs and groaned.

"Christ, you two are a fucking pair." Kent shook his head and chuckled. "Hell, my brother is going to blame me for this. God damn it all to hell. He's going to swear it's my fault the two of you are hurt, you know? And, he's a real pain in the ass when he has something to lord over me. Fuck. Come on, let's go before we get run over by the guys from NYFD."

They stepped out onto the sidewalk, just as the first fire trucks slid to a stop out on the street in front of the building. He could see Juan and Lakyn standing halfway down the long block near an ambulance and hoped Juan managed to get her out of the building unscathed.

Juan's muscular arm was wrapped around her waist, and it looked as if he had Lakyn picked up off the ground— no doubt trying to keep her from rushing back toward danger. He knew she was worried about her brother and probably him as well, but he wanted her to stay where she was. He shook his head when he saw her arms flail and her mouth running a mile a minute. Chuckling to himself, he bet Lakyn had just blown all the progress she'd made cleaning up her language.

"Can either of you hear what our woman is shouting down there? Damn, it looks like she's racking up punishment points right and left."

Kent coughed to cover his laughter at the looks they were getting as they helped the shouting, battered, and bruised man down the street. Thank God it was New York, and the passersby giving them curious looks wouldn't give any of them a second thought once they'd moved on.

Just another day in the jungle.

JUAN HAD BEEN pacing the considerable length of the hospital's waiting room for over an hour, waiting for news about Lakyn and Trac. Christ, he'd even counted the number of square tiles, he'd been so desperate for a distraction.

Lakyn had been fine when they'd run from the building, but one look at Trac's bruised and bloodied face as Kent and Cooper helped him out of the burning building, and she'd fallen over a curb, spraining her ankle so badly, they'd had to x-ray it to be sure it wasn't broken, and she'd gotten a nasty cut on her palm he was sure needed stitches.

Trac was suffering from a significant concussion and would likely be held at least overnight if the nursing staff didn't kill him. His hearing had already started to improve by the time he was wheeled through the double doors by two waiting orderlies. Thank God he'd stopped shouting at everyone—a little of that had gone a long way.

Juan had never been in a hospital yet that operated in a timely fashion, but that wasn't helping his patience. Damn, if he didn't hear something about Lakyn soon, he was going to take the place apart looking for her, and that wasn't going to end well for anyone. Turning his attention to Cooper, he listened as he and Kent reviewed what little information they'd been given by local law enforcement. No one understood why the team had cleared the lobby and floor where Lakyn was scheduled to meet the photographer and several members of her staff but minutes later walked into a trap.

Kent pulled his phone from his pocket when it beeped. "What have you got?" Juan was familiar and comfortable with Kent's terse communication style—once a SEAL, always a SEAL. "Remotely or on-site?" There was a pause before he abruptly disconnected the call. Juan saw anger flashing in Kent's dark eyes when he turned his attention to those gathered around him. Several other team members had joined them when they heard him answer his phone.

"Somebody accessed the elevator's control panel, sending Lakyn two floors above the one we cleared." Kent's anger was practically vibrating around him.

"Of course, they knew we would clear the floors above and below the one where she was supposed to meet the photographer." Sam McCall was standing nearby and sounded as frustrated as Juan felt.

"*And* since they changed the location two hours before the appointment, they knew we wouldn't have time to clear the entire building." Juan could see the stress on Cooper's face as he'd spoken. Hicks was becoming more and more frustrated with his inability to keep his sister safe—a sentiment Juan understood all too well. Cooper shook his head as he appeared to be casually taking in everything around him.

"There's a piece missing and as soon as I know my sister is safe, I'm going hunting."

Everyone on the team knew who Cooper would be looking for—Reggie Parks. Lakyn's manager seemed to have dropped off the map after his phone call with Kyle West. His sudden disappearance made everyone question his level of involvement, and personally, Juan suspected the son of a bitch was playing both sides against the middle—a game that would eventually turn deadly because he doubted there was a hole on Earth deep enough to elude Cooper Hicks.

A nearby door banged open, and a nurse pushed a wheelchair holding Lakyn into the room. The young R.N. looked frazzled and frustrated while her charge looked like she was seconds from going thermonuclear. Rushing forward, Juan and Cooper surrounded the women. As her brother, Cooper was able to deal with the dismissal paperwork—though Juan suspected the young nurse would have handed the sheaf of papers over to anyone willing to take the mutinous model off her hands.

Kneeling beside Lakyn's chair, he brushed his fingers down Lakyn's pale cheek and smiled. *"Cariña,* I'm so relieved to see you. I've been worried what was taking so long."

"I'd have been out here a lot sooner if Hitler's protégé back there," she pointed over her shoulder at the nurse who rolled her eyes, "would have let me walk out. But no, she has to give me a twenty-minute lecture on why the hospital can't assume the responsibility for me walking on one side of the door, but they don't care if I pretend to be an Olympic gymnast on this side. Have you ever heard of anything so ridiculous? Cripes, no wonder medical care is so flipping expensive, I'm sure it takes time to brainwash people to this level of absurd."

He had to fight his smile when he realized she was heavily sedated. Her pupils were dilated to the point there was only a very thin ring of violet still showing, and her words were beginning to slur.

"I want out of this chair." Her petulant expression almost made him lose the battle to hold back his grin. Damn, she was so cute when she was annoyed. Pointing at her ankle, she rolled her eyes in a delightfully exaggerated way,

"The boot is overkill. *Serious overkill.* Doctors are always overly cautious with celebrities because they think we'll sue them. I'm going to sue his paranoid ass for putting this *fugly* thing on me when an ace bandage from the local pharmacy would have been fine."

"You refused the elastic wrap for your hand." The nurse's annoyance was easy to hear in her clipped tone.

"You were going to charge me fifty-seven dollars for a three-dollar item. Mercy, it's no wonder affordable health care is out of reach for so many people. That markup is even greater than interior painters. Did you know their markup is estimated at over six thousand percent? *Six. Thousand. Percent. That's criminal.*" She was beginning to slur her words so badly, Juan was having trouble understanding her, and he frowned at the nurse.

"What did you give her?" The young woman had the good sense to look sheepish as she rattled off the name of several medications, one of them he recognized as a powerful sedative he suspected they'd given her more for their peace than her comfort. Kent West stepped forward crossing his bulging arms over his chest and glared down at the nurse as Juan picked Lakyn up from the wheelchair. Moving to a nearby chair, he settled her on his lap and smiled when she sighed and cuddled against him like a purring kitten.

Kent's body language was so out of the ordinary for the man known for charming women rather than using his considerable size to intimidate, Juan had wanted to pump his fist in the air knowing West had stepped up his game in Lakyn's defense.

"How much and when?" Kent West had been a medic in the SEALs, and his expression darkened when the nurse gave him the dosage information and time. The woman grabbed the paper Cooper had just finished signing and gave the wheelchair an expert spin before rushing out of the room. "They probably expected some pansy-ass agency employee to show up, so they drugged her to make her compliant."

Juan was furious but schooled his expression as he picked her up in his arms. Upsetting her further wasn't going to help, and she was fading fast, so he didn't want his anger to be the last thing she remembered. Kent's expression softened as he looked into her sleepy eyes.

"They loaded you up, didn't they sweetness? Did they give you an injection?" At her nod, Kent cursed under his breath. "As soon as we get the word on Trac, we're taking you to a secure site, and" he didn't get to finish because Lakyn started struggling to get off Juan's lap. Before Juan could get her under control, Kent's stern voice crackled like lightning.

"Stop! You are safe and so is Trac. We've got someone with him, and as much as it chapped the head nurse's ass, our guy is armed to the teeth." He shook his head and sighed. "We don't get this grief in Texas; our people know you don't protect bombing victims with words and a slap on the hands. I swear this city is desensitized to the point of being a fucking free-for-all."

Juan laughed at the Texans obvious dislike for New York. "The world would be a very boring place if everyone liked and believed the same things, Kent. Haven't you heard the old saying about variety being the spice of life?"

"You'd do well to keep that expression to yourself around my wife, or you'll find yourself on the same sinking boat with Cooper." The man in question chuckled beside them and nodded.

"I'm already scheduling the delivery of gifts to Tobi

while I'm in Washington for de-briefing. Hopefully, she'll have forgiven me before I return to Texas to officially join the team."

Juan laughed because they all knew Tobi didn't hold grudges, but she wasn't going to turn down gifts either. Juan watched as Kent refocused his attention on Lakyn and smiled at her loopy grin.

"We'll make sure you see Trac before we leave, sweetness. I can assure you, we're facing a similar battle trying to keep his ass here until the doctor clears him. His family is supposed to be in town soon, and we'd like to have you out of here before they arrive." Lakyn looked confused, but Juan knew exactly what Kent was talking about. The Hughes family was as cold as Juan's was warm, and the first time Lakyn met them, she needed to have Trac by her side to help her navigate frigid waters.

Chapter Twenty-One

COOPER SLIPPED PAST the security officer manning the front desk of Lakyn's apartment building, grumbling to himself about the elderly man's distraction. Taking the elevator to Reggie Parks floor, he was once again amazed by all the security blind spots. There were far too many places the ill-placed cameras missed, and anyone with any training at all would be able to use those to their full advantage.

Timing himself, it took less than ten seconds for him to open the door and step inside. If the man didn't give a rat's ass about his own safety, Cooper wondered how vigilant he'd been with Lakyn's. Stepping into the cool, dim space, the first thing Cooper noticed was the sense of emptiness. The furnishings were still where they'd been the last time he'd paid the prick a visit, but the space *felt* empty.

Any good Special Operator could tell you when they entered a space whether there had been anyone there recently. There was an energy shift when a space hadn't been occupied for a while. You could write it off as new age juju if you wanted, but it was a simple fact—people leave behind residual energy, it fades over time, but never completely leaves. Grateful he'd slipped on gloves before calling the elevator, Cooper began poking around, looking for anything that might tell him where Parks had gone—it didn't take long.

COOPER LEANED BACK in the oversized, black leather office chair and stared, lost in thought as he looked out over the twinkling lights of the city. He'd never been overly fond of large metropolitan areas, but if you had to spend time in one, a penthouse suite so far above the hustle and bustle of the street was definitely the way to do it. After spending more than a decade in some of the most dangerous and impoverished cities in the world, he truly appreciated a view where people look like ants during the day and completely vanish at night was pure magic. Hell, they were so far above the city lights, he could see a star twinkle every now and then. It would be several hours before the sun rose behind the Statue of Liberty, but the steady stream of headlights on the streets below proved this city rivaled Las Vegas as a city that never slept.

Cooper had been surprised when he found a packet with Lakyn's name on it set out in plain sight in her manager's apartment. The man had clearly wanted to be certain it was found. Cooper had pushed it inside the black tactical jacket he wore and continued searching Reggie Parks apartment for any additional clues. The man was nothing if not neat, so it had been easy to see he hadn't taken anything but the absolute essentials. Hell, if the building superintendent sent a crew to clean out Parks' place, they were going to take most of it home. The man's closet was filled to overflowing with designer label clothing that would yield a small fortune on the street. Shaking his head, he looked at a shoe collection that likely cost enough to feed a third world country for a year. *If you had that much money to spare, why didn't you let it do some good, asshole?*

One of the first things Cooper noticed when he entered the gaudily decorated space was Parks had emptied every trash bin in the apartment, a detail most people would never think of unless they'd been trained in covert operations. The one thing Parks missed was a small box he'd probably dropped in his rush to leave and accidentally pushed under the edge of the bed. The cardboard was from a disposable phone and included inserts with enough identifying information, Micah would be able to find and track the phone. There was an empty folder labeled *Passport & Documents* in the top desk drawer, saving Cooper the time looking for items he'd already been certain the man had taken. He didn't find any luggage in the apartment and the backpack Cooper knew the man used was also missing.

He hadn't taken time to look through the contents of the manila envelope Parks had left for Lakyn until he'd returned to the safe house, and what he found had both shocked and saddened him. The scuff of boots on the other side of the room pulled him out of his musings. Cooper turned his chair in time to see Kent West settling in a nearby chair.

"Awfully late—or early, depending on your perspective—to be up." Cooper gave the other man a questioning look. Why was West up and dressed at two o'clock in the morning?

"I don't require as much sleep as some people." Kent's casual shrug didn't fool Cooper. Most former Special Forces operatives had trouble sleeping—they'd seen and done too much for their subconscious mind ever to be completely free of the memories. "It was damned handy when the twins were newborns and will be handy again when the new baby arrives."

"Congratulations, I'm sure you and your family are excited." Cooper hadn't held a baby since Lakyn and thinking about it now made his eye twitch. Kent's soft laughter earned him a sheepish grin.

"I'd have expected better lying skills from a spook. Damn, you need to get out before you get your ass shot. At least most of our missions are rescues—quick ins and outs that don't require much time undercover. I'll make a note to keep sending Sage if a mission requires duplicity, that fucker could lie to God. Here's a tip, don't play poker with him or his lovely wife."

This time it was Cooper's turn to laugh. He liked both West brothers, but there was something about Kent that made the enormous man surprisingly approachable and easy to talk to. It was easy to see how Kent and Kyle had earned their reputations as skilled negotiators—they had the good cop, bad cop routine down pat.

"Duly noted." Cooper paused, searching the other man's face for a clue as to what prompted this awkward conversation. After several, long seconds of silence, Cooper arched a brow in question. "What's on your mind, Kent?"

Kent's heavy cowboy boot hit the floor with a resounding thud, and the big man leaned forward, resting his elbows on his knees. His considering gaze met Cooper's and he shook his head.

"I don't usually have this much trouble understanding *crazy* because frankly, it's easy to just chalk things up to the simple truth that most of the people we deal with professionally are just too fucking stupid to breathe and move on… but something about this mess doesn't add up."

"I agree. The man being hunted by the governments of several nations just happens to be on a small airliner that suddenly vanishes over the South Pacific without a trace?

Call me paranoid, but the whole thing seems awfully fucking convenient."

"Micah tagged all Parks' overseas accounts as soon as we knew his prints were on the listening devices in Lakyn's apartment, but so far, there hasn't been any activity since he went dark. There were some major cash transactions before he left the U.S., and Micah is still tracking those down, but there hasn't been anything since. Unless the man is a whole lot smarter than we originally thought, someone is helping him. Someone with a lot of connections and a deep desire to stay in the shadows."

And that, ladies and gentlemen, is the understatement of the year.

LAKYN STARED OUT the window into the night sky and wondered if she'd ever be able to sort out all the emotions surrounding the revelation Reggie had been working for everyone but her. In all honesty, that wasn't entirely true, he had worked for her at least on a superficial level. She'd lost his loyalty early in her career, and she kept racking her memory for a reason. What could she have done to merit such deception and betrayal?

"*Cariña*, you are thinking so hard, you are going to give *me* a headache." Juan smoothed his hand down her side, tantalizing her bare skin as his fingertips stroked from beneath her breast all the way to the middle of her thigh. Retracing the path, he wrapped his warm fingers around her hip and rolled her over until she lay flat on the bed beside him. Leaning close, he loomed over her, his stare focused and knowing.

"You're trying to figure out what you did wrong, aren't

you?"

She felt tears fill her eyes and much to her relief, he didn't scold her for the sudden display of emotion. Blinking away her tears, she smiled when Trac's face also came into view. She'd been opposed to him refusing to stay overnight in the hospital, but now she was grateful he was here.

"Princess, please don't cry, Juan's words weren't a criticism. We just understand how you think." Trac's eyes still showed the lingering shadows of pain, but he'd insisted the ringing in his ears was gone, and it would be easier to cope with the slight headache if he was away from the constant noise of the large medical center.

"Trac is right. As a submissive, it's your nature to please others, and being liked is directly linked to caring for other people. When others don't return their devotion, true submissives take it personally—very personally. It's hurtful and sends them searching for the answers to a plethora of *why* questions. What we're trying to tell you is you are not responsible for his behavior. Reggie Parks made the decision to sell you out. He sold out Cooper and his country, and the irony is he is running from those who could have protected him."

Lakyn knew Reggie would soon be facing several charges because he'd accepted money from a foreign nation in exchange for planting the bugs in her apartment. When they hadn't yielded the promised results, the coward had tucked tail and run. Micah Drake and Phoenix Morgan's facial recognition software and the cell phone information had allowed the Prairie Winds team to track her former agent as he made his way to the other side of the world. The men didn't know she'd overheard the conversation they'd had while they believed she was in the shower, but she was holding those cards close to her chest for now.

"I don't need this kind of publicity and neither do you. Your families have successful businesses... I don't want them to be damaged by your association with me." Both men recoiled as if she'd slapped them. Trac looked at Juan and shook his head in obvious frustration.

"I don't think we've made our intentions toward this woman clear enough, brother. Perhaps she needs a few pleasant reminders of how much she means to us?" The moonlight brought out the dancing mischief in Trac's eyes, and she fought the urge to roll her own eyes... something that had earned her more swats than she thought she deserved over the past few days.

"I agree, although I must confess being mystified by her confusion. I thought we'd emphasized the point several times during our flight to New York." The timbre of Juan's voice dropped, and Lakyn felt her body heat at the mere mention of their time in the bedroom of the Hughes Oil jet. They'd introduced her to the mind-blowing pleasure of ménage and given her what they called a stepped-up membership into the mile-high club. She felt her cheeks flush and wondered if they'd be able to see in in the moonlight.

"Jesus, Joseph, and sweet Mother Mary, I want to feel you between us again so badly, I'm about to lose my mind." She smiled at the way the two of them so cleverly diverted her attention to more pleasant topics. He tapped the tip of her nose with the end of his warm finger and smiled. "But you, my lovely sub, *are* very noisy when you come. Even with Juan's mouth sealed over your luscious lips and the jet engines roaring outside the window, it still wasn't enough to fully cover your tantalizing screams of pleasure, Princess. I'm absolutely certain the walls of this penthouse will not offer us the privacy we need." She moaned in frustration, and he chuckled. "Master Juan, I think our sub has gotten awfully greedy, what do you think?"

"FUCK, I HOPE so because I can barely think of anything else. Sliding as deep into her silky heat as I can get trumps everything else. I want to take you back to Texas and make love to you under a starlit sky, *Cariña*. Seeing your bare skin bathed in moonlight as shooting stars pass overhead will quickly become one of my greatest pleasures, I promise you. I want to introduce you to my family, so they can get to know the woman I've fallen in love with." This time Juan was happy to see those mesmerizing violet eyes swimming in unshed tears because he knew these were tears of happiness.

Juan's family would love Lakyn. Her soft heart, giving spirit, sense of humor, and work ethic would all be points in her favor—but ultimately, it would be the joy she'd brought into his life that would endear her to the loud and loving Riveras.

Trac would also introduce Lakyn to his family, but they would like her for entirely selfish reasons. Her fame rather than the woman herself would be the only thing they'd see. Juan had always been amazed that a family with so much had never seen how little it meant without love.

Chapter Twenty-Two

TRAC WASN'T PROUD of the fact he'd felt nothing but relief when he'd learned the plane carrying Reggie Parks had gone down. He wasn't going to pretend to feel grief for a man who didn't have a fucking clue what it meant to be loyal.

There hadn't been any reason to add to Lakyn's emotional burden tonight, so they planned to tell her about Parks tomorrow—tonight was about giving her a chance to process the contents of the letter he'd left her. None of them believed the letter had really been for her. Reggie Parks' infatuation with Cooper Hicks had been the driving force behind every move her manager had made for years. Bragging to anyone who would listen about their greatly exaggerated friendship had ultimately painted him in a corner and led to his downfall.

Every covert operative in the world knew their family and friends were potential targets—hell, that was the reason they protected their family's anonymity at all costs and most operatives had few if any friends outside professional circles.

Trac and Juan would help dry her tears, but he wasn't sure how many she would shed for a man whose friendship had been a sham from the very beginning. Turning his attention back to the woman in question, he pressed his lips against hers in what he'd intended as a quick kiss, but when she threaded her fingers in his hair giving it a quick tug, fire exploded in his groin.

Her hot tongue slid along the seam of Trac's lips, and he opened with a growl before wresting the control back from the little hellion, twisting his head to gain deeper access to the sensitive recesses of her mouth. Seducing Lakyn when they had to stifle her responses was the sweetest torture in the world. The crinkle of a condom wrapper was his signal to move. In seconds he was painting her lips with the tip of his weeping cock. Seeing the pre-cum glistening on her kiss-swollen kips was hotter than hell.

"I'm going to fuck you until you are too exhausted to stare out into the dark, worrying about things you cannot control and are not responsible for, *Cariña*." Juan's voice was rough with obvious arousal, and for the first time he could remember, Trac wished his and Juan's positions were reversed. Watching his friend slide his arms under Lakyn's legs, lifting them until her knees were draped over his elbows, opening her pussy to their view made his cock jerk in response. He'd never balked at the term fuck, but Lakyn brought a tenderness out in him he hadn't known existed. Making love to her under the Texas sky would be everything Juan mentioned and more.

LAKYN RELISHED THE sensations humming through her sex. Juan swirled the tip of his cock through the soaking wet folds of her pussy, giving her a wickedly sexy smile. She loved Juan's playful nature and his innate sensuality, just as she loved Trac's dominance and strength. Knowing both men wanted her was empowering.

Since meeting them, Lakyn had been continually surprised how rarely they mentioned her physical appearance. For as long as she could remember, Cooper was the only one who saw her as more than a pretty face, even her parents had seen her as little more than a money-making entity. She'd loved them, but once her face had started earning money, she'd stopped being their little girl and become their meal ticket.

She'd overheard Juan and Trac's earlier conversation with Cooper and Kent about Reggie and understood why they planned to wait to tell her that her former manager was presumed dead. What they didn't know was she didn't care one way or another, at this point. Learning he'd only dealt with her to get closer to her brother hadn't come as a huge surprise, but it had burned the last remnants of the bridge of friendship and mutual respect between them. She wouldn't wish harm on anyone, but in her mind, he'd already been dead, so knowing it was a reality wasn't a big change.

"*Cariña,* it's a bit disheartening to know your mind is wandering when I am a split second from pushing my aching cock balls deep into your heat." Juan's growled words brought her back to the moment, and she felt her face heat in embarrassment.

"I swear I'd flip her over and paddle her ass, but she'd enjoy it too much." For once it was Trac who sounded amused, but when she reached a hand for him, he shook his head. "No, Princess, if you wrap your soft fingers around my cock, this will be over far too soon." Tapping the underside of her jaw, he grinned. "Open up and let me have that beautiful mouth. Let's see if we can't get you to focus, what do you say?"

The instant her hot mouth closed around Trac's cock,

Juan flexed his hips, pushing himself between the swollen folds of her slick pussy. Juan's groaned at the burning heat gripping him. Arcs of electricity traveled up his spine before settling in his balls. Gooseflesh prickled along the surface of his skin, and he sucked in a deep breath trying to hold back the urge to fuck her hard and fast. Juan felt his eyes rolled back and heard Trac's chuckle just before he groaned. *Serves you right for laughing at me, fucker.*

"Fucking hell, your mouth is pure heaven, Princess. I can see by the look on your other Master's face, he thinks the same thing about your hot pussy—absolute perfection and OURS." Juan slid his cock out of Lakyn's pussy, enjoying the wet sounds as her body tried to hold him in her heat. The walls of her vagina were already quaking with spasms around him as her body anticipated the pleasure. Trac pulled in a deep breath before he found his voice again.

"Fuck, yeah, baby. That perfect bit of sucking you do with your mouth mimics the way your pussy grips a cock, and it's almost too much to endure."

Juan was being swamped by pleasure—blinding ecstasy he swore was beyond anyone's ability to put into words. The only piece he could single out was the possessive part of his soul that sent up a silent prayer, pledging to never let her go. Lakyn belonged to them, and they belonged to her. The logistics of where to live and how their careers could all work together wouldn't stand a prayer as an obstacle to the love between them.

All of those details were for another day—this moment was for loving the woman who had blown into their lives and proven the best things in life come to you in those moments when they are least expected.

Epilogue

Six Months Later

REGGIE LEANED BACK against the warm wood of the shaded beach chair and looked out over the crystal-clear water. The steady lapping of low waves as the tide moved in lulled him into a relaxed state he could ill afford. It wouldn't be safe to let his guard down until the last surgery was done. He'd undergone two rounds and was awaiting the third.

He wasn't allowed time in direct sunlight, but the clinic staff finally relented and let him enjoy a few minutes outside each evening. Reggie knew he wasn't a particularly cooperative patient, but this small bit of fresh air each day helped and was likely the only reason the staff had been willing to bend their rigid rules.

Walking by mirrors always caused made him do a double-take, a habit the staff warned him he needed to break as it would be a red flag to anyone trained to read body language. The strangeness of seeing another person staring back from a mirror would likely be an exercise in confusion for a long time. Not recognizing the person staring back at him, Reggie often caught himself staring into reflective surfaces, wondering if he'd ever be able to put into words how strange it was to meet the eyes of someone he knew hadn't existed six months ago. *The doctors keep telling me I'll eventually get used to it. I'm putting my trust in them and hoping like hell it's true.*

He let his mind wander to Cooper Hicks and wondered what the other man had thought when he learned he'd been dealing with a man working for multiple agencies and not been any the wiser. Reggie was an agent—but not the entertainment agent everyone had believed him to be. One more surgery and he was going after the man who'd seen him as little more than a glorified babysitter.

The next time when they met, things would be different...

The next time, Cooper would be his—one way or another.

The End

Books by Avery Gale

The ShadowDance Club
Katarina's Return – Book One
Jenna's Submission – Book Two
Rissa's Recovery – Book Three
Trace & Tori – Book Four
Reborn as Bree – Book Five
Red Clouds Dancing – Book Six
Perfect Picture – Book Seven

Club Isola
Capturing Callie – Book One
Healing Holly – Book Two
Claiming Abby – Book Three

Masters of the Prairie Winds Club
Out of the Storm
Saving Grace
Jen's Journey
Bound Treasure
Punishing for Pleasure
Accidental Trifecta
Missionary Position
Another Second Chance
Star-Crossed Miracles
Dusted Star

The Wolf Pack Series
Mated – Book One
Fated Magic – Book Two
Tempted by Darkness – Book Three

The Knights of the Boardroom
Book One
Book Two
Book Three

The Morgan Brothers of Montana
Coral Hearts – Book One
Dancing with Deception – Book Two
Caged Songbird – Book Three
Game On – Book Four
Well Bred – Book Five

Mountain Mastery
Well Written
Savannah's Sentinel
Sheltering Reagan

The Christmas Painting

I would love to hear from you!

Website:
www.averygalebooks.com/index.html

Facebook:
facebook.com/avery.gale.3

Twitter:
@avery_gale